THE RATASTROPHE CATASTROPHE

THE ILLMOOR CHRONICLES

BOOK ONE

THE RATASTROPHE CATASTROPHE

DAVID LEE STONE

interior illustrations by
BOB LEA

HYPERION BOOKS FOR CHILDREN

NEW YORK

First Edition

1 3 5 7 9 10 8 6 4 2

Designed by Christine Kettner

Printed in the United States of America

Reinforced binding

Library of Congress Cataloging-in-Publication Data on file.

ISBN 0-7868-5128-7

Visit www.hyperionbooksforchildren.com

For my mother,
Barbara Ann Stone

SELECTED DRAMATIS PERSONAE

(ye cast of characters)

BARROWBIRD: A distant relative of the forest hornbill

BURNIE: Troglodyte councillor

CADRICK, TACITURN: Trade Minister

FINLAYZZON, GODRICK: Owner of Finlayzzon's inn

FIREBRAND, CHAS: Owner of the Rotting Ferret tavern

FORESTALL, TAMBOR: Council Chairman, ex-sorcerer

FRANKLIN, VICTOR: Assassin

GOLDEAXE, GORDO: Dwarf mercenary

GREEN, MIFKINDLE: Assassin

GRIM, BERNARD: Ratcatcher

MARSHALL, PEGRAND: Manservant to the Duke
of Dullitch

MICK: Mite

MODESET, VANDRE: Duke of Dullitch

PHELT, CEDRIC: Militiaman

PIDDLETON, TOMMY: A lame boy

QUARRY: Lord Chancellor of Dullitch

QUICKSTINT, JIMMY: Thief/herald; Tambor's grandson

SANDS, QUARIS: Home Secretary and member of
the council

SIDDLE, MALCOLM: Ratcatcher's apprentice

SOAK, ROCHUS: Seer

STUMP: Adventurer

TEETHGRIT, GROAN: Barbarian mercenary

VICIOUS: Fox terrier

WUSTAPHA, DIEK: Charmer

WUSTAPHA, MRS.: Farmer's wife; mother of Diek

WUSTAPHA, PIER: Farmer; father of Diek

THE
RATASTROPHE
CATASTROPHE

D URING THE TRI-AGE (civilization's third attempt at getting things right) there grew, on the swollen lip of the continent of Illmoor, a city quite unlike any in recorded history.

The rulers of Dullitch were imbecilic, and their incompetence gave rise to such diverse crimes as fraud and murder. Among the nobles, one vile family after another struggled for power, submitting their sons as prospective lords in order to strengthen their stake in the city. On the tenth day of every tenth year, a new duke was chosen, each invariably more corrupt and

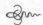

untrustworthy than the last—"A snake to lead snakes," it was said. Under such leadership, which allowed a vile assortment of assassins and pickpockets to thrive and squirm beneath it, the city quickly earned a grim reputation. It became despised by many and generally avoided by travelers through the Gleaming Mountains, by which it was sheltered, like the treasure hoard of a particularly insecure dragon.

And what a horde Dullitch contained: humans, trolls, ogres, sprites, elves, pixies, dwarves, gnomes, giants, and greenskins. Remarkably, considering the sheer diversity of races, a lasting peace endured.

Still, a large, weather-beaten plaque swung back and forth on tired hinges above the city gates, proudly welcoming all and sundry to visit Dullitch. Though a local saying warned, "You haven't lived until you've visited Dullitch and, after that, you won't want to. . . ."

The continent of Illmoor is riddled with magic. Not the empty, inept magic practiced by men who believe themselves to be members of the Ancient (now defunct) Order of Sorcerers. This is the original, undiluted magic from which the continent itself was constructed: a powerful and volatile force that has leaked out through the ages, rising up from the graves of long-dead warlocks.

Two types of magic coexist: *light* and *dark*.

Light magic finds its place in the air, giving rise to galloping unicorns, love charms, and fairy groves before it evaporates into the ether. It is a gentle and harmonious force, a force at one with nature. Though much sought after by amateur "sorcerers," it proves practically impossible to harness; and those who do spend long hours in pursuit of mastering it are often said to be deranged.

Dark magic, on the other hand, seeks immediately to earth itself in the land it was once used to forge. Arising from the long-dead souls of great and terrible enchanters, it is an angry magic, an untamed source, a parasite yearning for a host.

And hosts are rare.

Trees suffice, for their roots go deep, but this is no way for dark magic to travel; when it lodges itself in trees, the results are straightforward, rather boring, and nobody gets hurt. No, what dark magic truly requires is susceptible minds. These are a delicacy and, although seldom encountered, are always relished. But dark magic is a reckless lodger; it cares little for the minds it invades.

A particularly powerful charge of dark magic appeared during the reign of Duke Modeset. Though it would affect the lives of several very different people, it arrived almost entirely unnoticed. In fact, only two pairs of eyes in the whole of Illmoor observed its passage.

These belonged to the mercenaries, Groan and Gordo, although their part in the story would not become apparent for some time. Long before they had the notion to set their steeds southward, the magic had found its mind.

A searing wave of energy infiltrated a land of fields and forests, seeking the warmth of a weak mind, homing in, until . . .

ONE

W*HOOSH...*

Diek Wustapha dropped his flute. The leather-bound book that had been resting on his lap tumbled to the floor and lay open, its pages flapping in the breeze.

"What is it, lad?"

The boy turned and looked up at his father, his smile was apprehensive. "I thought I heard something, Dad."

"That'll be the cattle cart," said his father, quietly grateful that his son had stopped playing; Diek's musical ability suggested possible employment in the torture trade.

Mr. Wustapha looked out over a broad expanse of west-country farmland, his brow creased. A few cows in the field opposite had wandered over to the gate and were mooching idly about.

"No, it was more like a feeling than a sound. I thought I *felt* something."

"Well, that'll be your dinner," his father continued, reflecting on years of terror at the dinner table. Mrs. Wustapha was one of a long line of cooks on her mother's side of the family. He hoped fervently she would be the last. "You know something, boy, when I first met your ma, she used to make puddings the like of which would turn your stomach inside out for days on end."

"Yes, Dad. So you've told me. Repeatedly."

"Fair enough. You're reading again, I see?"

Diek nodded, sliding his flute under a rock with the heel of his boot. He snatched up the book. "It's called *Ancient Royal Fables*."

"Good lad," said his father, patting the boy affectionately on the shoulder. "Have you got to the bit where Huud the Wise tells Prince Kellogg to go round up the sheep?"

"No, Dad."

Diek looked up. His father was waiting patiently, a grin spreading across his broad face.

"I'll go and round the sheep up now, Dad," he said, with a knowing smile.

Diek got to his feet and set off toward the north field. His father watched him go.

Diek wasn't a bad lad, he thought, at least, not in the conventional sense. He just dawdled from time to time, lacked direction. Perhaps he *should* take his brother's advice and send Diek to Legrash for the summer, let him experience a bit of the real world. What harm could it do?

He stroked his chin thoughtfully, wondering exactly how much trouble a young boy could get into in a town like Legrash. A boy like Diek. Probably best not to speculate. He whistled a merry tune and headed off to see how his son was getting on with the sheep.

The magic sank into Diek's mind like a stone plunging down a deep well. There it lay low, biding its time with patience born of millennia lingering in deep caverns, lurking in dormant hollows.

When the magic decided to surface, it did so with such reptilian guile that no human eye could detect the change. Diek Wustapha, however, was cursed with the ownership of a barrowbird with particularly keen sight.

The barrowbird is a curious creature indeed. One of the High Art's darker throwbacks, it was rumored to have once been an ordinary scrawny relative of the forest hornbill. Legend holds that on the few occasions throughout history when the gods decided to visit Illmoor, they did so by inhabiting the minds of barrowbirds. On one such occasion, it is said that one particularly spiteful god decided to leave something behind: the curse known as *Vocalis Truthilium*, commonly translated as "I speak as I find."

And the barrowbird did just that. In fact, it gave a new and terrible meaning to the phrase. No personal comment was beyond it. Despised as a species, its put-downs included such harsh observations as "You'll never get a girlfriend unless you actually cut that ear off," and the oft heard "If I had a figure like yours, love, I'd stay indoors for the duration."

Now Diek's own barrowbird was treating him to a baleful stare. "There's somethin' amiss with your right eyeball," it chirped. "'S glowin' like an ember, ain't it?"

"Is it?"

Diek blinked and raised a hand to his head. He'd been propped against one corner of the pigpen all morning, watching the truffle hogs misbehaving. "Maybe I'm coming down with something," he said, beginning to wander off around the side of the pen. "I *do* feel a bit odd."

He reached for his flute and brought the instru-

ment to his lips, but was interrupted before he was able
to muster a tune.

"Could be fouleye," the barrowbird squawked.
"You hear of a lot of folk dyin' from that."

"Dying? It's fatal?"

"Right as mustard. You ask anyone: 'How's your
daughter, Milly?' 'Fouleye took her.' 'How's your
aunty Ethel?' 'Down with fouleye.' One minute you
can be runnin' around in a field, the next you're a
goner. That's usually the females, mind. I never heard
of a male taken with it yet."

"Okay, okay. It's probably not that, then."

Diek produced a single, shrill note from the flute,
then stowed it away in his tunic. He didn't feel much
like playing today; his heart really wasn't in it.

He sighed and closed his eyes tight, then tentatively
opened them again. "Has it gone?" he asked.

"Has it, heck!" said the barrowbird. "Now they're
both alight! Well, stone me. You're not standin' on a
lightnin' rod or somethin', are ya?"

Diek took a step back, then looked around. "I'm
not standing on anything," he said. "Besides, you
noticed it when I was over there."

The barrowbird put its head on one side. "Then, if
I were you, I'd go and see the apothecary or, come to
that, the village witch."

"I need to do my chores. Besides, why would I want to see a witch?"

"Well, first there's the eye thing, and then maybe you could find out why you're suddenly such a magnet for the pigs."

"Huh?"

Turning about on his heels, Diek noticed for the first time that all twelve of his father's hogs had followed him along the length of the pen and were now squatting in a group just beyond the fence. Curious. Usually, they ignored him completely, unless he had scraps. "Th-that's odd."

"Odd ain't the word, boy. 'F y'ask me, you're up the creek without a shovel."

"I think that's supposed to be a 'paddle,' and I feel fine, *thank you*. Now, I'm going to see to the milking . . . *alone*."

The barrowbird hopped onto a nearby tree branch, and watched Diek skulk toward the milking shed. "Somethin' amiss," it muttered. "Somethin' amiss, right enough."

The milk was curdled. Rather, it hadn't been curdled when Diek had first picked up the bucket, but it was definitely curdled now.

Diek tipped the bucket, shaking his head as a series

of fat, creamy blobs plopped onto the bench below. Odd. He took a step back, turned on his heels and stopped dead. All the cows were staring at him, their tails swishing in the shadows of the milking shed. There was definitely something wrong; they usually took no notice of him whatsoever.

Maybe it *was* time to see an apothecary. . . .

Diek's visit to the apothecary wasn't entirely successful. The man, like most of the villagers, largely ignored everything Diek had to say, before supplying him with a strange potion that looked and tasted like seven-year-old jam. He was to take it three times a day, as instructed, or alternatively, whenever he "felt a bit odd." The old man certainly hadn't given him any useful advice, and quickly changed the subject when his flowers wilted as Diek got up to leave. On reflec tion, Diek had practically been thrown out of the shop, in the end.

Diek had always been a loner, but now he took to spending whole days in the fields by himself. He had decided to give the barrowbird to his father as a birthday present; its insults and depressing forecasts of hideous eye disorders had become unbearably tiresome. Also, it had started crowing about Diek's increasingly resonant voice and made a pointed comment that, every time he played a note on the flute, the neighbor's grimalkin came tearing across the Midden Field as though the hounds of hell were after it.

He *had* seen that wretched cat a lot lately.

Weeks passed and, as the magic took root inside Diek's mind, it began to surface in a peculiar fashion, giving the boy an almost magnetic personality. His foolish absentmindedness became thoughtful contemplation; his inane and idiotic comments were replaced by clever and insightful witticisms. In short, people of Little Irksome began to notice Diek Wustapha.

They would spend a few moments talking with him, then trail after him in large groups, like sheep after a shepherd. This was all much to Diek's astonishment; he'd never had a lot of time for people before. Now they praised him and appreciated his music (unlike his father, who only tolerated the odd tune every evening after tea). These people wanted more. They would wait quite patiently all day, just on the off chance of a tune. It wasn't that his music was particularly melodic, as Diek would have been the first to admit. On the whole, it tended to comprise a few strangled notes huddling together in mournful misery.

Then, one afternoon, everything changed.

Diek had been playing for Butcha, the baker's niece, when suddenly the music came alive. He didn't even notice it happening; it was simply there at his lips, awaiting release. To the girl's mesmerized delight, he produced tune after tune, melody after melody, song after song. These delicate pieces floated into the air, twisting and turning in the breeze, and were carried for miles over the hills and dales. Slowly, one by one, the villagers of Little Irksome stopped what they were doing and craned their necks to listen. Then they put down their tools and washboards, snatched up their hats, and fastened their walking shoes. The cobbled lanes of the village were suddenly alive with curious people irrevocably drawn to the sound.

By midafternoon, the entire population of the village stood grouped around an oak tree in the Midden Field, listening to Diek Wustapha weave his tunes. And play he did. From that day forth, he knew that nothing in his life would ever be the same again.

So did his parents.

In practically no time at all, Diek's talents had become many, from snake charming to hypnotizing mice. Visitors arrived from a few of the neighboring villages to watch his skills and hear his music. Deep inside his subconscious the magic was throbbing, turning, gaining momentum. And he carried his flute wherever he went.

He'd taken to playing long, drawn-out melodies too, whimsical at first, and then, as the days drifted by, progressively stronger. Melodies could be more than mere tunes, he discovered. Melodies could be almost magical.

Diek found himself reflecting on things like the reception of spiritual messages, the existence of telepathic sheep and, more important, his part in the larger scheme of things.

"Everybody's got a place in the big picture, lad," his father would say. "It's just a matter of finding out where you fit in."

Diek wondered where he *would* fit in, and found himself gazing longingly toward Dullitch, capital city of Illmoor, with its gleaming spires and megalithic monuments.

TWO

IT WAS SUMMER in Dullitch, the air was clean and sobering, and the streets were filled with the combined odors of freshly baked bread and exotic spices. In the marketplace, throngs of hungry patrons lined up for the early bargains, and a few rogue mongrels gathered for free pastry offcuts at the baker's serving hatch.

It was the annual Clairvoyants' Awareness Weekend and a fete was being held in tribute to Ouija Mastook, the oldest (and most incontinent) medium on record.

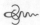

The guest of honor was due to arrive at midday and no one knew what to expect. The bandstand was currently being reinforced to withstand the weight of Mastook's entourage of nursing staff.

Usually, the ceremony consisted of a rambling speech, three (extraordinarily loud) cheers, and several rounds of celebratory drinks. Invariably, it would conclude with a séance in which somebody's aunt Margaret turned up to let them know that her valuables were hidden in the attic.

Atop the Church of Urgumflux the Wormridden, two members of the dreaded Yowler cult were taking turns peering through a spyglass at the proceedings below.

The Brotherhood of Yowler was indeed the stuff of nightmares. It was a ruthless organization rooted in the worship of dark gods who demanded the theft of priceless treasures and ritualistic executions to sustain their life force.

The Yowler cultists were cloaked assassins, thieves, and cutpurses, but their presence in Dullitch was endured because several of the city's founding families were members. These midnight rogues were extremely well paid and enjoyed considerable support from the City Council, who turned a blind eye to corrupt Yowler-run associations.

Mifkindle Green, a junior Yowler member, was

"wasping." This meant dropping in at any large and important gathering, planting a sting (that is, assassinating the most prominent person there), and clearing out quickly to avoid capture. His colleague, Victor Franklin, a known night-runner and poison-dart specialist, was drumming his fingers distractedly on the stonework.

"W-w-will you stop that, Vic?" snapped Mifkindle.

"What? Oh, sorry, I just wondered why you hadn't fired yet. You're usually in and out in a cat's sneeze."

"Shhh. Can't you k-k-keep quiet? You've been so judgmental since you k-k-killed old Banks in that g-graveyard run."

Mifkindle's gaze returned to the scene, but he wasn't looking down toward the fete. He was staring intently at a small cottage garden on the opposite corner of the street.

"What is it?" Victor persisted, anxiously. "Have we been spotted? Is it the militia? *What are you looking at?*"

"R-r-rats."

Victor boggled. "Come again?"

"R-r-ats," Mifkindle confirmed. "There's a l-l-line of them heading into the DeLongi place through a g-g-gap in the front wall."

"Yeah, and?"

"They're w-w-walking in s-single file, like an army. It's odd," he said, with conviction. "And I've seen a l-lot of them r-recently. Almost every d-d-day, in fact."

Victor shrugged. "Dullitch is a big city. You gotta expect rats."

"Not l-l-like th-these," said Mifkindle, pursing his lips as he passed the spyglass across to his partner.

"B-b-big, aren't they?" Victor said, after a pause.

Candleford School for Boys stood proudly on a slight rise in the northwest corner of the city. It was usually a place of high activity, breaking glass, and enthusiastic blasphemy. Now, however, during the summer holidays, the place was quiet.

In a room crammed with stoves and piled high with crockery, Bernard Grim, the ratcatcher, applied half an ear to the wall and listened intently. His apprentice, a boy named Malcolm, with rugged features and a black eye, watched with mounting trepidation.

"It could be a field mouse, Mr. Grim."

"Don't be ridiculous, lad," Grim growled. "You don't get field mice in a workhouse kitchen. Who ever heard of such a thing?"

"My uncle had one come into his kitchen," answered Malcolm.

"Your uncle's no better than he should be."

"Do you think it could be a rat?" piped up a short, plump maid with golden ringlets and a porkpie smile.

"Aye," said Grim, wondering about the unconcealed eagerness in her voice.

"Ain't nothing wrong with my uncle," said Malcolm sulkily.

Grim ignored him and leaned in closer, raising a finger and tapping tentatively on the woodwork. A scratching began on the other side of the wainscoting.

"He might be eccentric," continued Malcolm. "And I know he talks to himself a bit, but he's never done anyone no harm. Well, apart from that Mrs. Haveshank, and she said she wouldn't be pressin' charges."

"Quiet, lad! It's on the move; listen!" said Grim.

The apprentice knelt down beside his employer, face creased with the effort of concentration. Eventually, he gave a reluctant nod.

"Right," Grim whispered. "Get me a forty-seven from the cart."

Malcolm crept out of the kitchen and returned a few moments later, laden with an assortment of wooden planks. "I couldn't remember which one was which, Mr. Grim."

He passed a plank from the stack to the ratcatcher and waited patiently as Grim balanced it in the palm of his hand.

"That's a sixteen."

He handed back the plank and rolled his eyes as the apprentice chose another. "That's a one-seven-four."

"But they're identical, Mr. Grim."

The ratcatcher turned to the maid and offered her a wry smile, but found no sympathy in those eyes. The woman's face was distinctly odd; it looked as though there was far too much space between her brain and her mouth. Grim returned his attention to the wainscoting, and found himself hoping the rat had managed to escape.

"Are there cellars below, miss?" he asked.

"There used to be," the girl said, nodding. "The principal had them all blocked up when a few of the teachers were caught tutoring after hours."

Grim focused on the flagging wallpaper. For the first time, he spotted a large yawn in the wainscoting. "Would you mind leaving us alone now, miss?" he managed. "This little experiment shouldn't take long."

The maid gave a slight nod, lifted her apron and hurried away. The curious smell that Grim had noticed on the way in seemed to depart with her.

"She didn't look too clever, did she?" the ratcatcher whispered conspiratorially. "I reckon she's been at the stock or something."

The apprentice looked mystified. "Why d'you say that?"

"Well, there's a funny smell from her. Didn't you notice it?"

"I did, as it happens. I just didn't like to say anything; I thought it might be those scones you had for breakfast."

Grim studied the young man's expression for a few moments, and then hit him with the one-seven-four. After offering the boy a vicious scowl, he returned his attention to the wainscoting, and froze.

A pair of glowing red eyes was staring back at him. They were attached to the largest rodent Bernard Grim had laid eyes on in more than twenty years in the trade.

"M-m-malcolm," he managed. "Forget the wood. Get a dagger."

Afternoon came and went.

"Apprentice to Bernard Grim the ratcatcher, milord."

The palace guard bowed low and stepped to one side, admitting the scrawny frame of the ratcatcher's assistant. At the opposite end of the long hall, a thin, angular-faced man sat scribbling furiously behind a desk laden with paperwork. He didn't look up when the door closed behind his trembling visitor. "Sit."

The command echoed around the hall. Eventually,

the man behind the desk stopped scribbling and popped the pen into an inkwell. Then he looked up. "Not on the *floor*, boy! Get a chair, for heaven's sake."

The apprentice moved quicker than the eye could see, snatched up one of the chairs, and pulled it toward the desk. Then he tucked his cap into a back pocket and sat down, embarrassment playing across his face like sunlight on a pond.

"Now," said the duke. "You wanted to see me about something?"

The boy nodded.

"Well?"

"We caught a rat, milord," said Malcolm, nervously.

"Really?" said the duke, proffering the smile he generally reserved for lunatics and tax evaders. "And that's unusual, is it?"

Malcolm frowned and reached up to scratch his chin. "In what way, milord?" he asked.

"Well, unless I'm very much mistaken, you are a ratcatcher. Surely snaring the odd rodent is all part and parcel of the job, no?"

"Not when they're this size, sir."

The creature the apprentice proceeded to pull from his trousers was quite unlike anything Duke Modeset had seen before. He leaped from his seat and yanked the chair in front of him. He had no desire to suffer the frenzied death leap of a half-expired monstrosity.

"Oh, don't worry, milord," said the boy, reassuringly. "It's a goner. But there are more of them, we reckon. That's why I've come to see you. They've built a base beneath Candleford School. We heard 'em, this morning. They start goin' at it, they could be all over Dullitch in minutes. I know the council's supposed to deal with this sort of thing, and I did try knocking at City Hall, but I don't think anyone's available."

"Oh?" said Modeset, eyebrows raised.

"There was this wooden board outside the door. It said, 'Gone Fishing.'"

Modeset let out a long sigh. When reflecting on the council's overall performance of late, "Gone Fishing" seemed to be an accurate description.

"These, er . . . these rats. There could be an awful lot of them, you say?"

The apprentice nodded. "Mr. Grim, that's my gov'ner, he reckons that if you let it go more than a week you're gonna have to paint whiskers on the royal crest."

"I see. Thank you, young man. That will be all."

He dismissed the boy and summoned his servant. After a few moments, a man came hurrying into the room. He was short and stocky, with long hair (though none on the top of his head), a well-groomed beard, and a fixed, sort of bemused smirk. "What is it, milord?" asked the servant.

"Pegrand! We have something of a crisis on our hands."

"Oh gods, no. What is it, the chef?"

Modeset sighed, plucking a copper coin from the tabletop and employing it to scratch the bridge of his aquiline nose. "No, Pegrand, not the chef. Don't get me wrong: I don't like him and he has to go, but this time it's something a little more serious."

"Okay, milord. I'm all ears."

"Good. Do you remember those fellows from the watchtower patrol who fell in here last week mumbling something about a rat horde beneath the Poor Quarter?"

"Vaguely, milord," Pegrand said, dismissively.

"Have them arrested immediately!"

"Er . . . right, milord. Any particular charge?"

"Oh, I don't know. Causing a disturbance of the peace? Malicious lies? I'm sure you'll think of something."

"Of course, milord. Is there a problem?"

"Yes, perhaps. There does, in fact, appear to be a rat horde beneath the Poor Quarter, and I don't want any I-told-you-so's stirring up the conspiracy theorists."

Pegrand Marshall scribbled a note on the pad permanently suspended on a chain attached to his belt.

"Er, won't the act of arresting two watchtower guards stir up the conspiracy theorists, milord?"

"Mmm? What? Well, oh, yes, I suppose it will. What do you suggest?"

"Well, we could rub them out, dump the corpses up past Gate Field, and then have two boys from the plough crew carve out a crop circle round 'em. That way we might have the conspiracy theorists up in arms, but at least they'll have something baseless to talk about."

"Excellent. Meanwhile, however, we do have a serious problem. This morning's little visit follows three from the merchants, two from the sewer attendants, and several from the Yowler Brotherhood, all with news of rat sightings. An outbreak is imminent."

"I'll put the palace on high alert, milord. Anything else I should be doing?"

Modeset nodded gravely. "Go down to the riverbank and round up the council. Tell them we have an infestation of giant rats that, despite its humble beginnings, could have designs on the Merchants' Quarter. That should get them suitably anxious. Oh, and let them know time is short; we need a publicly acceptable announcement by Friday evening."

Modeset took a deep breath, waited for the servant to flitter away, then caressed his eyelids with the rough tips of his fingers. It was obviously going to be one of those days.

Morning arrived to find a grim scene at City Hall.

The Dullitch Council members stared gloomily at one another over the long debating table. They had been called to the Gray Room at an unspeakable hour and were waiting to shout at anyone who looked even partly responsible.

Eventually the acting chairman, Tambor Forestall, appeared in the doorway. Tambor had been dreading this moment ever since his predecessor had vacated the premises over a month before. It was just so typical of his luck. For three years Gambol had chaired Dullitch Council and, in all that time, there had not been a single catastrophe or even a mild uprising. *He* gets the job and, whizz, a plague of giant rats.

He wasn't being helped by Duke Modeset's latest initiative demanding "A Council Structure Reflecting the Ethnic Makeup of a Modern Society" either. He cast a worried glance around the room, noting with horror that only four members of the council were human. He recognized a local alchemist, but the barbarian was a total mystery, and the cross-species squabbling in the corner, he'd already decided to file under "Politely Ignore." There were definitely a few goblins in there somewhere, and possibly even a wood gnome.

A vein throbbed in Tambor's temple and his arms were aching, but it was too late to back out now. He banged his gavel hard on the tabletop. "Gentlefolk!" he began.

"*Gadjfjr—*" said a squeaky voice nearby.

"We have been called here today—"

"*Gktgngn gkkrg jfjf kfg fjy—*"

"On a matter of the utmost urgency."

"*Gghfhfh fkfkf frjfjfj.*"

Tambor hesitated, driven to distraction by the echo that seemed to accompany his every utterance. Sitting beside him at the table was a warty, green-skinned midget with long, pointed ears and teeth in various stages of decay. His nose looked like a melted candle, and a strange green mucus dripped from the end to the tabletop. It occurred to Tambor that he'd never seen this creature before. "Excuse me," he ventured. "Who *are* you?"

The creature sighed. "I'm the translator."

Tambor leaned forward conspiratorially.

"For who?" he said.

"The orc down at the far end," said the midget. "He doesn't speak Plain Tongue."

"What language *does* he speak?"

"Brave. Not that you can call it a language, as such."

"No Brave translation for 'terrible infestation,' then?"

"No," said the midget, shrugging noncommittally. "Not unless you can squeeze it into words of one syllable."

Tambor appeared to consider this. "Fair enough," he said. "How about 'rats'?"

He leaned back and smiled contentedly.

The rest of the council began to sit up and exchange a few concerned glances.

"Right. Everyone listening?" said Tambor forcefully.

"Rats, you say?" shouted a seer, from the far end of the table.

Tambor glared at him. He had a personal dislike of seers for a number of reasons, not least because their largely invented profession had outlived sorcery in Dullitch. Also, they regularly insisted on fanciful names like "Izmeer of the Swarm" and never seemed to achieve anything that didn't require a lot of skulking about in caverns with a piece of chalk and a far-off look in their eyes.

The seer glared back at him, correctly reading his

expression. "Sounds jolly intriguing," he said, and turned away to finish his game of cards with the goblins.

Tambor watched him quietly, then returned his attention to the remainder of the City Council. He wished, quite fervently, that he had taken the job at Jimmy Stover's pie shop. Only Quaris Sands, the elderly Home Secretary, seemed to be paying any attention, though he was mumbling incessantly under his breath, clearly put out by the early call. Tambor groaned. "All right, everybody," he said wearily. "We have a plague of giant rats in Dullitch. It started beneath the Candleford Boys' School, and it's growing by leaps and bounds. The Poor District is already in dire straits and the Merchants' Quarter could be next. All the ratcatchers have fled in terror, and even the assassins have declined the contract. We're looking to devise some potential solutions to offer to his lordship, Duke Modeset."

The translator raised his hand. "How about sending in a big cat?" he said.

"I don't think you're actually on the council," said Tambor. "Anybody else?"

The translator offered him a scowl, and leaned across to inform the orc representative that Tambor had just insulted its mother.

"It could be an omen from the gods," said Taciturn

Cadrick, the trade minister. "A sign that we should seek spiritual and intellectual fulfillment."

"So, what do we do about it, O wise one?" asked Tambor, mockingly.

"Don't ask me. Perhaps we should try hiring a mercenary to destroy them. How about that barbarian fellow from the Virgin Sacrifice Scandal?"

"No chance," said the Home Secretary quickly, shaking his head. "I wouldn't have that lunatic back inside the gates for all the gold in Spittle. It took us months to mop the blood off the clock tower. This city has suffered enough humiliation at the hands of mercen—"

The rest of his sentence was drowned out by the screams erupting from the almshouse across the street. The council hurried to the windows and looked down at the scene unfolding below. People were pouring out of the small doorway, trampling over one another and crying out for help.

One woman's screech was clearly audible amid the uproar. She was yelling at the top of her voice, "Rats! Rats! Raaatsss!"

As the council looked on, the writhing sea of humanity swarmed toward the marketplace, turned a corner and disappeared.

"All right," said Tambor, massaging an injury from

the council's mad dash to the window. "Let's have a vote of hands, shall we? One, two, four, eight—yes, I think we're pretty much decided. I'll get a message to the duke."

THREE

DIEK WUSTAPHA was watching three of the village girls watching him. Their names were Trist, Tadrai, and Dreena, and they had been following him across hill and dale for the best part of the morning. This was odd, Diek noted, because only weeks before, they had thrown a bucket of sheep excrement over him and called him names. Now they were trailing mere feet behind him, stopping when he stopped, eyes turning downward with a curious respect each time he cast a glance over his shoulder. Strange.

Still, the attention felt good: he liked the taste of it, the air of power it gave him. He wanted more. . . .

Of course, he had been carrying the flute. Although he hadn't actually been playing it, he supposed the slightest hint of a note had kept them with him.

He didn't know where this knowledge came from; he simply knew it to be true.

It was the same with sheep: they followed him everywhere. Then again, they were sheep, and sheep will eagerly pursue anyone who looks like they might have a vague idea of where they're headed. But it didn't explain the cows, horses, pigs, dogs, birds, lizards, and other, more nondescript creatures whose fixed attentions he had drawn during the waning week.

Diek came to a sudden stop, cast his gaze back to the group of girls and then down at the instrument resting in his palm.

Play. Won't you play? Won't you, Diek? Play.

The three faces were sullen, lips turned down, and no voice seemed to have risen among them.

Hesitantly, almost reluctantly, he raised the flute to his lips.

"Look at them cows. Now, there's a thing," the barrowbird said, as it flapped and squawked its way on to Pier Wustapha's shoulder.

Diek's father stood at the door of the cottage and looked out over his broad acres of farmland. Presently, his wife joined him, her face a patchwork of wrinkled confusion. "What're they doing, love?" she managed, aghast.

The question produced a shrug from her husband and a thoughtful scowl from the barrowbird.

"Beats me, love," said Pier. "It looks like they're making for the field nearest Olvi's place."

"Why would they do that, d'you think?"

Pier Wustapha shook his curly head. "I've no idea. There's nothing much over that way, apart from—"

His wife waited for an end to the sentence, but none came. "Apart from what?" she prompted.

Pier scratched at his bottom lip.

"Well," he said, uncertainly, "I saw young Diek go off that way this very mornin'. They could be followin' after him like Mibbit's dog and the cat as hangs around the farm. Seems like every livin' thing's taken after the lad. Even old Tyler's daughters were on the trot when I last spied 'em."

"Oh no." Mrs. Wustapha rolled her eyes. "Not them again! What *is it* with the lad?"

Pier lanced a boil with an overgrown fingernail. "He'll be all right in time," he said. "It's . . . er . . . it's probably just a phase he's going through."

Mrs. Wustapha frowned. She didn't look too sure.

"Play some more, Diek, won't you play some more?"

The words had definitely come from Dreena this time. Her sky-blue eyes were piercing his soul; he felt like a rabbit caught in the trapper's mechanical jaw, awaiting the inevitable. And all the while, a voice, The Voice, seared through his thoughts like a hot blade *You can have anything, Diek Wustapha, anything you want. All you have to do is—*

"Diek!"

His father's voice, distant but determined.

All you have to do—

"Diek, lad!"

All you have—

"Diek!"

A sharp slap burned his cheek, and Diek awoke from his reverie. The girls had drifted away to make room for his father, who was shaking him as if fearful that he might have descended into a swoon. As Diek came round, Pier Wustapha staggered back, looking at his own hand as if seeing it for the first time. He'd only given the boy a glancing slap, yet his hand felt as though someone had been sticking needles in it.

"That's it, lad," he spat, massaging his aching palm. "That's it, you hear me? It's time you went away from here, got yourself a place in the world. There's something badly amiss with you, boy, and I'm damned if your mother an' I are gonna get thrown out o' the village because of it."

$\mathbf{D}$UKE MODESET, reluctant ruler of Dullitch and its bubonic environs, reclined in his chair and gazed absentmindedly at the large family crest over the fireplace; a regular pool of rainwater appeared beneath it during every shower. It was a sign of the times. Recently, the payment of city taxes had become so rare that the palace staff had been forced to block up leaks with such finery. Even his marble throne had been an early casualty in the war against bad weather: it was now to be found atop the east tower, where it served as a weight for the antique trapdoor beneath it.

Modeset squinted, coughed, and yelled for the mail. Then, remembering the servants' favored delay in responding to commands, went to fetch it himself. The contents of the royal mailbox turned out to be three tax demands addressed to an unknown cobbler, an appeal for donations from the Church of Urgumflux the Wormridden, and a letter from Tambor Forestall, the council chairman, notifying him of the city's official line on the rat situation.

Modeset's hawkish features fell foul of a frown; it was very unusual for the council to put anything in writing, let alone provide multiple-choice solutions and several small boxes requiring the royal seal. Their new chairman must be quite the ticket. Slowly, however, the duke's smile returned. It appeared that the council leader had mistakenly dispatched the original draft of his letter which, bereft of secretarial corrections, read:

Dear Lord Madshat,

The council and I are fully aware that you are by way of being a little mentally challenged, so we'll avoid using long sentences in order to make this letter very simple.

City—Problem—

PLAGUE OF RATS

SOLUTION	POSSIBLE/KNOWN DRAWBACKS
I. *Hire a ratcatcher*	*There is not a ratcatcher in the entire city*

	who'll go near a job like this with a ten-foot barge pole.
2. *Send in the militia*	*Of our 1,004 militiamen, 1,000 are currently deployed in the mountains of Mavokhan in our war against Phlegm, and the other four are off sick.*
3. *Burn affected areas*	*This is not really a solution, as burning down all affected areas of the city would leave just the palace and Joe Donn's Bakery.*
4. *Hire mercenaries*	*No drawbacks. Mercenaries do just about anything for the right price, and several of the household names are known to be at large in the hills around Dullitch at this time.*

Best wishes,
Tambor Forestall, Chairman

Modeset finished reading the letter, sighed, and rang for his manservant. Pegrand Marshall arrived with characteristic lethargy, a silver platter in one hand and, for reasons probably best left unknown, a plunger in the other.

"You rang, milord?" said Pegrand, bowing his head before the duke.

Modeset was shaken from his reverie. "Mmm? Oh,

yes, so I did. Get my carriage, will you? We need to pay a long-overdue visit to City Hall; it appears the council has drawn up a selection of possible actions against our rat crisis, and they require my seal."

"I see, milord," said Pegrand. "Does that actually demand a personal appearance?"

"Mmm? No, it does not. However, I have chosen the option of hiring mercenaries and I would like to ensure that our good friends in the council recruit the, how can I put it, correct breed of scumbag for the job. Does that sound right?"

"Absolutely, milord. After the Virgin Sacrifice Scandal—"

"Exactly," said the duke, shivering at the memory of that disaster.

"What was that heathen's name again, sir?"

"Umm, Teethgrit, I believe; a suitably heinous name. Shall we go?"

FIVE

WaNTeD
FOR
Crimes Against
Alchemy

Leaven Grismal

Reward if believable
explanation given to
Society of Alchemists

DEEP BENEATH Dullitch, the rodent tide
began to swell. Driven on by the urgency to feed, the
rats tumbled over one another in their haste to reach
the surface, forming a terrible frenzied carpet that
flowed inexorably upward. Despite the twisted maze of
the sewers, the rats swept along with an eerie purpose,
veering at every junction, scratching at every grate.
The carpet of vermin seethed on: thousands of tiny
legs scrambled insanely toward their distant goal, while
rows and rows of gleaming teeth chattered longingly
for sustenance. . . .

The city awaited.

❋ ❋ ❋

The Dullitch North Gate was hemorrhaging heralds. They rode forth in every direction, each one privately more determined than the others to return with the city's savior; each one secretly wondering just how much of the reward money he could pocket.

First out of the gate was a gangly, greasy youth named Jimmy Quickstint. He rode the fastest, youngest, and most agile of the horses, though, because of his natural inferiority complex, he thought it the cripple of the bunch. Jimmy had, in an illustrious career spanning more than three years, worked as a baker's assistant, an apprentice alchemist, and as journeyman to an insane toy maker with designs on world domination. He currently spent his nights bidding for membership of Yowler's elite thievery consortium. His days were spent serving burned fry-ups at Spew's Breakfast Bar. Occasionally (on a Wednesday afternoon as a rule), he also found time to be a city herald.

Jimmy didn't know very much about horses. Indeed, he was so focused on staying astride his beast that he had little or no idea that he was a good mile ahead of his nearest rivals. He had even less of a clue that two of Illmoor's most infamous mercenaries were leaving a village along his current path and he would soon be accosted by them. Some knowledge you can do without.

The road out of Spittle was notorious. It wound its way along the floor of a wide valley surrounded by lush and verdant woodland. Here and there ancient standing stones would mark rises in the road, an idea employed by Duke Modeset's predecessor toward the end of his reign to ensure the safe passage of Dullitch's lumbering war wagons. Despite the fragrant air and sweet serenity of the surroundings, no one except the poor or suicidal ever traveled this way; the road was a notorious breeding ground for bandits.

Gordo Goldeaxe put his head to one side and squinted. A poster was nailed to one of the trees, fluttering in the breeze. He jumped up and ripped it down. "'Wanted for Crimes Against Alchemy,'" he read, gripping the poster in his chubby little hands. "'Leaven Grismal. Reward if believable explanation given to Society of Alchemists.'"

Loud footsteps approached, and a sword was stuck into a patch of ground beside the tree. A palm the size of a melon gripped the dwarf's shoulders and lifted a stout battle-axe off its half-rotted strap. It had been hanging precariously for the last half an hour, and Groan was tired of watching his small companion struggle with it.

"Thanks," said Gordo.

A nod.

"Looks like your typical idiot gold brewer," the dwarf continued, attempting to read the small print on the poster with little success. "Don't suppose there's much money in it."

His companion said nothing.

"Is there something wrong with you, Groan?"

Gordo looked up at a man of immense proportions. Muscles jostled for position in every limb, like snakes trying to escape from a sack. He was absolutely massive, and would have struck terror into the hearts of most living beings, had it not been for the crocheted bobble hat that perched atop his head like a cherry on a cupcake.

"You've been miserable all week," said Gordo, removing his helmet and tucking it under one arm. "Ever since you saw that magic rainbow thingy just past Irksome."

"Yeah, well, you know 'ow it is," said Groan, turning his bulbous head skyward. "I don't trust magic, specially when it comes from the clouds. 'S bad enough when we 'ad sorcerers firin' off spells left, right, an' center, now we've got magic comin' outta the sky. Can you 'magine what'd've 'appened if that blast 'ad hit us?"

"Well, it didn't," snapped Gordo, impatiently. "It hit some stranger down in the valley."

Groan frowned. "How'd you know that?"

"I saw it through the telescope," answered the dwarf as he stuffed the poster into his belt. "I didn't show you because you were waving that sword around like a lunatic. Oh, and speaking of lunacy, Groan, where exactly did you get that hat?"

"Killed an orc up near Scoon," said Groan, flossing his teeth with a length of twine. The warrior gave great attention to his teeth and—when engaged in combat—to those belonging to other people. "This hat was all he had on him."

The dwarf appeared to consider this. "Couldn't you just have left it there?" he asked.

The warrior tried to shrug off the observation, but Gordo was undeterred by Groan's attempt to avoid giving a straight answer.

"What *is* it? Why the hat?"

When it came to taking hints, the dwarf wasn't the quickest of companions. The only drifts caught by his family were the kind you had to remove with a shovel.

Groan stared down at Gordo long and hard. Then he removed the hat. The hills echoed with laughter.

"How did *that* happen?" said Gordo, once he'd managed to regain control of himself.

"You remember that dragon up at Vale Wake?" said Groan, flushing with embarrassment.

"You said it missed you," said Gordo, still smirking as he gazed at his friend.

"I lied," said Groan, crestfallen.

There were approximately ten hairs left on Groan Teethgrit's once lock-laden scalp.

"Cheer up," said Gordo, patting the warrior companionably on the kneecap. "Could be worse."

Somehow, the statement was less than convincing.

"Horse up ahead," said Gordo, changing the subject. "Maybe more than one. You know what that means?"

"Aye," answered Groan. "It means we'll 'ave somethin' to ride to the next village."

A sudden flash of inspiration brought the dwarf to a standstill. "I've an idea! Why don't we just go back to Spittle and take that air balloon the locals were mucking about with?" he said. "There's no reason to kill these riders; we could just storm the square and . . . what?"

Groan raised one eyebrow, a particularly expressive gesture for a man whose discourse was usually limited to a succession of grunts. He shrugged.

"What I mean is," Gordo continued, "we can't attack on the road. Remember? The only folk who use the road these days are thieves and the local militia, and we can't afford any more trouble with Dullitch, not after that mess-up with the Virgin Sacrifices. I still have nightmares about *that*. Whereas, if we get the balloon . . ."

"I ain't gettin' no b'loon," said Groan, emphatically. "B'loons is for clowns, an' I look like enough of an idiot in this hat."

"Oh come on, buddy. At least think about it," pleaded Gordo.

Groan gave the situation a moment's thought. It was over in seconds. "We'll attack the riders," he said. "That's what they're there for."

"I vote we find out who it is, first," said Gordo.

Groan shook his head. "I wanna fight," he said. "An' kill folk."

"Right, fair play. So that's one vote for you and one for me, giving me the majority."

A confused expression crossed Groan's face.

"Remember how I told you to work it out?" added Gordo.

The horse was slowing; having been present at a number of notable land wars, it had an instinct for trouble. However, Jimmy Quickstint didn't know this, so he dug in his heels and tried to urge it onward.

Suddenly, there was an obstruction in the road. At first Jimmy took it for a mountain troll, but then he noticed the crocheted bobble hat and the leopard-skin posing pouch. Another distinguishing oddity, on closer inspection, appeared to be a barracuda tooth on a nipple ring.

"First, get off the 'orse, or die," it said. "Then you can 'and over all yer gold, or die. You'll 'ave noticed that two of them . . . er . . . six options is you dyin'. Make yer choice."

Jimmy brought his horse to stop (at least, he meddled with the reins a little; the horse had actually stopped moving a few minutes before).

"What do you want?" he asked, fearing another options-based summary of the situation.

Groan looked momentarily taken aback. He wasn't used to having to repeat himself.

"Hang on, I know you!" Jimmy continued, his voice edged with genuine glee. "You're Groan Teethgrit, the barbarian who got thrown from the Crest Tower after that business with the virgins!" The thief slapped his thigh, gave a little whistle and grinned like a hyena. "What happened to that fat one-eyed dwarf you used to hang out with? What was his name? Cordy?"

"Gordo," said Gordo, emerging from the thick

undergrowth beside the path. His planned entrance had been rudely interrupted by the thief's description of him as a "fat, one-eyed dwarf." "And I'd thank you to keep personal remarks to a minimum while I'm carrying this battle-axe. You'll find that protects against accidental decapitation."

Jimmy held out his hands in a conciliatory gesture. "I don't want any trouble," he said, the corners of his mouth turning nervously upward. "In fact, I've been looking for you two. That is, looking indirectly. I bring an important message from Duke Modeset and the Dullitch Council. It's a message for several local mercenaries. Dullitch has been infested by a plague of giant rats. We need someone to go into the sewers and wipe them all out."

"What's the pay like?" Gordo said, almost before Jimmy had finished speaking.

The thief considered lying about the reward money, but quickly thought better of it. Instead, he whipped a scroll from his saddlebag and unfurled it. "Says here twenty gold crowns," he began.

"Twenty? But that's absolutely—"

"Per rat," Jimmy continued.

There was a momentary silence.

"Plus a thousand crowns reward money for disposing of the entire horde."

There followed an even longer pause.

"This mercenary list . . . how, um, how many names have you got on it?" said Gordo, speaking slowly and carefully.

Jimmy performed a quick finger count. "Seven," he said eventually. "You, your friend, Sven Sussussafson—"

"Dead." Groan interrupted. "Taken out by a dragon on the Loft Rise."

"Okay." Jimmy nodded. "I'll cross that one off. Er . . . Ffaff Qumray?"

Gordo shook his head. "Mutilated by a skeleton horde up near Skoquement; terrible thing for a man to go through, 'n' all. They actually sawed his leg off, usin' his other leg."

"I see. Well . . ." Jimmy continued. "Then we've got Porridge Riley."

"Orcs, I'm afraid," said Gordo, making a face. "An absolute barbarism; they only ever found an ear."

"Stabb the Brave?"

"Over a cliff in Chudderford."

"Cordwyn Styke?"

"Wife did him in."

Jimmy sighed deeply and gave a dismissive shrug. "Well, that just leaves you boys," he muttered, looking up from the scroll. "Will you come?"

Groan and Gordo glanced at one another.

"We might be able to fit it in," said the dwarf.

Jimmy made to snatch up the reins, then hesitated.

"There's only one problem," he said.

"Yeah, what's that?" asked Groan, always ready for a confrontation. His few remaining hairs bristled.

"Well, there's only this one horse, and it can't really take all three of us."

"That's not a problem," Gordo said, and shrugged. "You can walk back."

SIX

MEANWHILE, the news of Dullitch's swelling rodent infestation began to spread. The rumors started innocently enough, as all rumors do. Bernard Grim, the ratcatcher, was quick to swear his hapless (nay, *hopeless*) apprentice to secrecy but, as fate would have it, Malcolm talked in his sleep. He also shared rooms with Thomas Dimchurch, above the baker's shop in Furly Lane.

Thomas, a member of the notorious Rooftop Runners, was the very soul of discretion. His strict

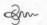

code of ethics meant that he would keep a secret to the grave. However, he had recently tripped on Malcolm's discarded sandal and broken his leg, incapacitating him and forcing him to withdraw from a date with Trissa Lefyette. So, in a moment of anger and frustration, he repeated the apprentice's mutterings to Chas Firebrand, the owner of the Rotting Ferret tavern. In all probability, that was the turning point.

Chas had a mouth; it wasn't a big mouth but it was a mouth with ambitions. Anything you told Chas could be relied upon to stay between you, himself, and just about anyone else the man laid eyes on.

Within a few days, word had spread from Dullitch and its swarming environs, to the far corners of Illmoor.

Dullitch is under attack. Dullitch is under siege. Dullitch is infested with . . .

"Rats?" Diek Wustapha raised one chiseled eyebrow in mock amusement. He'd left his home in Little Irksome for the neighboring town of Crust with his parents' blessing, a week's worth of bread and cheese, and enough gold to afford him shelter. "But rats are relatively harmless, aren't they?"

The villager he'd been talking to boggled at him, noticing for the first time that the boy's eyes glowed like burning coals. Still, an idiot was an idiot. . . .

"Haven't you ever 'eard of the Great Fire of Dullitch?"
Diek nodded. "Of course."

"Well, it was rats what pulled that off. Well-known fact."

"Hmm . . . I thought a baker started it," said Diek.

"Yeah, but some folk reckon he was a rat by day," whispered the villager.

Diek thought about this and decided not to pursue the matter. The fact was that there appeared to be strong rumors of a hostile infestation in Dullitch, and the capital city of Illmoor was bound to have a sizeable treasury. You didn't need to be a mathematician to count the odds. "And people are frightened, you say?"

"Oh yes, terrified," the villager continued. "Word is, they're afraid to walk the streets and they're too scared to stay inside, because the rats are coming through the floorboards. That's mainly them who's poor an' lives by the downstream. O' course, uptown all the rich 'e plannin' a big ol' protest on account o' findin' out what the duke an' the council are gonna do 'bout it all."

"I see. How do you know all of this, exactly?" asked Diek, trying to sound casual.

The villager offered another shrug and pointed east toward the town hall.

"Heralds," he said simply. "Two arrived from the

city this morning. Of course, I'd already 'eard most of it through the grapevine by then."

Go now, urged The Voice. *Enlist. You can make . . . a difference.*

Diek looked around him. He'd planned to stay a little longer in the village, but now, on reflection, there didn't seem to be any point. Dullitch beckoned, and Diek felt compelled to entrust himself to fate . . . and to the voice that seemed to call him, ever so gently, to task.

Diek abruptly dismissed the villager, who thought better of taking offense, and made his way over to the town hall. As he disappeared into the distance, the villager noticed that the patch of grass on which the boy had been standing had burned clean away.

Evidently, Dullitch's infestation hadn't drawn that many eager potential saviors. In fact, out of the five men present to sign up for mercenary duties in the Crust Town Hall, only Diek had all his limbs. Still, it seemed that a lifetime passed before the other hirelings staggered, hopped, and clawed their way through the line.

Diek swallowed, tightened his grip on the flute, and stepped up to the seated herald.

"Name?"

"Diek Wustapha."

He tried hard not to watch the herald's bushy eyebrows mating as he scribbled Diek's name down with a
quill.

"Division?"

"What are you babbling about?" answered Diek,
sharply.

The herald leaned back in his chair and folded
both arms.

"If you're a mercenary, you have to fit into some
sort of category."

"Such as?"

"Well," said the herald, impatiently. "Such as
assassin, warrior, barbarian, mercenary, extermina-
tor, vermin expert?"

"I'm none of those things!" huffed Diek.

The herald was beginning to look mildly annoyed.
"Then how, young lad, do you propose to rid our city
of rats?"

"Using this," said Diek, proffering his flute.

"What is it?"

"My flute," answered Diek, proudly. "I play, people follow."

"Just people?"

"Animals too. Donkeys, horses, rabbits. Even . . ."

"Rats?"

"Yes, of course!"

The herald nodded. "Then you're a charmer," he said. "I don't think we need—"

The herald suddenly stopped speaking. It was as if an invisible hand had gripped him by the throat. His skin turned a milky white color, and his hands began to scribble almost automatically.

"A charmer, excellent," he said, gasping to catch his breath. "Sounds good to me; it's certainly worth a try."

Then he put the quill down and shook his head. "Um, you're the only charmer, so far," he managed, in a more level tone. "You can come back to Dullitch with me. I'll send a cart for the rest of the sign-ups, not that it's worth it." He rolled up the scrap of parchment he had been writing on and gestured toward the mercenary who had clawed away just before Diek had stepped up. He was still only halfway to the door.

The heralds weren't messing about. They had been given specific instructions and a nonnegotiable time-frame in which to achieve them. Within a few minutes of signing up for the cause, Diek found himself thundering toward the distant spires of Dullitch on a horse that seemed oblivious to any obstacle until they'd actually hit it. When the herald eventually indi-cated a resting point in the middle of Bunkly Wood, Diek had to spend three-quarters of an hour plucking thistles and snapped-off branch ends from his neck and chest. The horse seemed fine.

Duke Modeset was staring down his nose, a frequent habit after any length of time spent with a member of the Dullitch Council. Having dropped in at the City Hall and found them all out "on civic duties," he decided to dispatch a handful of road wardens with the task of retrieving at least one official and bringing him, her, or it to the palace. They had located Tambor Forestall in double-quick time, dragging him (kicking and screaming by all accounts) from the gambling room of a local inn.

"So you sent word . . ." the duke began, "*before* you actually had my approval?"

"Er . . . yes, milord. I thought it would look bad for you if we dallied about. You know how it is with politics."

"Hmm . . . interesting. You've seen to things personally, I trust?"

"Oh yes. Absolutely!" said Tambor. "Heralds have been sent in all directions. Not merely in an attempt to recruit existing mercenaries, but also to scout for any other relevant . . . talentists?"

"There's no such word in the language," Modeset sneered.

"No, milord, but I'm sure you see what I mean."

Modeset nodded. He was of two minds whether to offer the man a drink (Forestall was edging dangerously close to the decanters), but decided against it on grounds of rumor. It was speculated that Tambor enjoyed his drink, often at the expense of a good suit.

"So," said Modeset. "I take it we'll hear from these heralds tomorrow."

"Heard from them yesterday," Tambor blurted, obviously regretting the statement as soon as it escaped from his lips.

"Excellent!" said Modeset, visibly shocked. "Any encouraging responses thus far?"

"Well, we've had three," said the chairman, producing a scrap of parchment and leaning over the desk to pass it across, "and we're still waiting on some of the slower carrier pigeons; a few of the newer heralds aren't that sure how to use them. All from outsiders, naturally."

"Hmm . . . yes, so I see." Modeset looked over at Tambor, squinted at the parchment, and continued. "I see we have the usual gaggle of knights from Bree, asking for half the kingdom and their expenses paid, a couple of mercenaries, and a young foreigner with a name I wouldn't even try to pronounce. . . ."

"We think you say it 'Dick,' lordship," said Tambor, helpfully.

"I see. There doesn't seem to be a title next to his name."

Tambor scratched his beard thoughtfully. "To tell you the truth," he said, concealing the urge to grimace. "We don't reckon much on that particular applicant."

"Why not?" asked the duke.

"He's just a young chap from the countryside," answered Tambor. "The boy reckons he can charm folk by blowing on his flute."

"In public?" Modeset said, aghast. "Surely there's some sort of law. . . ."

Tambor shook his head. "Strange folk, countrysiders," he muttered, as a few shards of daylight infiltrated the arched windows of the palace. "If you ask me, milord, they're all a bit haystacks."

"This report: it says here that these people actually follow him around. How extraordinarily eccentric."

Tambor gave a nod of agreement. "Quite a sight too, I imagine."

"Absolutely incredible," said the duke.

"It's not just the villagers, either," said Tambor. "Sheep, pigs, cattle, dogs, rabbits; they all trail after him, apparently."

"Could be he's got a magnetic personality," said Modeset.

Tambor nodded. "Well, he's certainly had an effect on the heralds," he said. "The one who sent this message gave his two-weeks' notice in with it."

"He resigned?"

"Yes. Must be an unsettling lad, eh?"

The two officials shared a moment of silence, as Tambor rummaged through the fathomless depths of his robe in search of a pipe.

"I'm assuming you don't want us to try a few more ordinary measures first?" said Tambor eventually.

Modeset smiled humorlessly. "What's the point?" he said. "We don't want to send in ratcatchers or assassins only to have them return with bubonic plague. Also, rather unhelpfully, our twitchy friends over in Legrash have refused all trade with us until some sort of resolve is assured."

"That bad, is it?" asked Tambor.

"It would seem so, yes. This proposed mercenary band is to be paid suicide rates for the disposal of the plague. Their coffer allocation is to be considered bottomless."

Tambor raised his eyebrows as a crash erupted from deep within the palace. A glass ornament toppled from the duke's grand mantelpiece and shattered. Evidently dinner was being served, or else the rats had reached the palace. Either way, it was time for him to leave.

❋   ❋   ❋

It was late afternoon in Dullitch and the crowds were beginning to ebb away. This was due in no small part to the two mercenaries striding down Palace Street. An air of impending doom surrounded them, but that wasn't unusual in Dullitch; anyone who didn't have that air was quickly arrested and executed (occasionally the other way around).

"Look at this: they're everywhere!"

Groan and Gordo were kicking rats out of the way with every second step. They had been told to head for the palace, where they would be "received with true Dullitch hospitality." Gordo hoped that this wouldn't be the case. He knew that "Dullitch hospitality" generally involved a three-hour wait in a dingy cell before some antique jailer arrived to spit a pardon all over them.

"I was thinking about that fight we had in Phlegm," he said to Groan, trying to take his mind off the palace. "I reckon we'd have won that and no mistake."

"Reckon you're right," said Groan. Groan had been in good spirits since he'd stolen a helmet from a quivering youth on guard at the Market Gate. He offered Gordo a gaping grin.

"Half an apple?" said a voice behind them.

"Anyway," Groan continued, ignoring the

interruption. "I don't reckon that baron was up to much. We'd 'ave 'ad to kill 'im."

"Granted," said Gordo. "There's plenty of those border lords that owe us a few bob. Take the fat earl from down Shade Way; we was more than fair with him, considering."

Gordo looked up at his companion. "You still got his head?" he asked.

Groan massaged his jaw and shrugged. "Dunno."

"Half an apple?" someone interjected.

The two companions parted, allowing a rogue wearing a rapidly expiring tunic and grinning like a stowaway cat on a fishing trawler. He gave them a two-fingered salute.

"Half an apple?" he repeated persistently.

"No thanks," said Groan.

"I'm not offering." The stranger frowned. "I'm asking. Have you got half an apple I could borrow?"

"Why half?" said Gordo, intrigued.

"Well, I didn't want to ask for too much."

"Why borra?" said Groan, indefinitely.

"Well, when I said *borrow*," the beggar continued. "I was speaking figuratively, like."

"So you want half an apple to *keep*?" asked Gordo, suspiciously.

"Yep, if it's not too much trouble. Now that you

mention it, I could let you have it back in a few days, but I don't suppose you'd want it."

"What would you do with the uvver arf?" said Groan, still loitering at the beginning of the conversation.

"He wouldn't have two halves, would he?" Gordo reasoned. "He'd only have the one half we gave him."

The beggar looked wretched. "Well?" he said eventually.

"Well what?"

"Can I have half an apple or not?"

"We haven't got one!" Gordo snapped.

The beggar was silent for a moment. Then he offered them an alternative salute and disappeared down a side alley.

Groan and Gordo arrived at a corner where a few of the outlying market stalls were packing away for the evening. The dwarf looked back over his shoulder and scowled as three cloaked figures shrank back into the shadows. He'd always had a distinct loathing for Dullitch, and this visit was proving no exception.

SEVEN

D

ULLITCH was seething with rats.

There were rats on the street, rats running along the window ledges, rats in the gutters. Diek couldn't believe his eyes: the legendary capital city had fallen to a new kind of enemy. No one could have predicted it.

You can remove them. Diek hadn't heard The Voice since he'd left Little Irksome. Now it spoke in a reduced, raspy tone; it was almost snakelike.

The herald reined in his horse and reached out for the reins of Diek's own beast of burden. "You can get off here 'n' make your own way to the palace. I'll need to check the horses back in."

Diek found himself practically shoved off his mount; he had to jump two rats and dodge a frying pan aimed at a third before he managed to catch up with the herald. "Aren't you going to take me to the palace?" he asked the herald. "No," said the man, suddenly more eager than ever to get away from his companion. "Duke's granted an audience to all mercenaries at five o'clock sharp. Don't be late."

"But I don't know my way around!" whined Diek.

"Your way around what?" asked the herald.

"The city, idiot!"

The herald boggled at him. "There *is* no way around the city, lad. Dullitch is an absolute maze. Just find a tavern and wait till five, then head for the palace. It's the big spiky thing in the distance."

Diek watched with bewildered rage as the herald urged the horses down the street, away from him. He gave a silent curse and wasn't entirely surprised when the man fell off his steed and tumbled into a pile of garbage bins gathered to one side of the street.

Hmm . . . amusing. Very amusing.

Diek looked around for a tavern. There didn't seem to be a great shortage of those. In fact, he could see only one building on the street that *didn't* look like a tavern, and that turned out to be a brothel. He wandered up and down the street outside the less rowdy bars (the ones that didn't keep ejecting drunks onto the cobbles) and eventually headed for a single, solitary door that sported a small wooden board proclaiming:

THE ROTTING FERRET
est. 824 / prop: Mr. C. Firebrand
Bring your own stool.

Please make every effort to mop up any
of your own blood.

Be careful as you go down; steps are very steep
(giants are advised to watch their heads,
dwarfs their arses).

This bar does not encourage fighting,
but actively supports it.

NOTHING TO SEE HERE.

Diek sighed; unfortunately, the Ferret was clearly the best of a bad bunch. He turned the handle and made to go in. As he did so, he felt a surge of sudden confidence. The voice was ringing in his ears.

Onward, it urged. *Down into the bar. They will cower before us.*

Groan Teethgrit and Gordo Goldaxe both had a life-time's experience with violent taverns. If asked to pick the most acutely evil drinking pit in the entire expanse of Illmoor, they would undoubtedly have settled on the Rotting Ferret. Death wasn't just a regular occurrence there; the business enjoyed a twenty percent discount at Domino's Funeral Parlor (located, rather conveniently, in an alley that paralleled the street on which Ferret customers tended to land face-first).

The place was a dive, an underground drinking pit that gave shelter to thieves, assassins, and a variety of other miscreants. It also boasted the largest mixed species clientele in Dullitch; there were elves, ogres, trolls, orcs, goblins, sprites, pixies, and woodlings. Occasionally, you even got the odd tooth fairy (though they seldom stayed until closing time).

Groan was having a very good day; first he'd seen an attractive barmaid, and then he'd been delighted to see Grid Thungus, a rangy barbarian who'd worked for the same warlord over in Legrash. Neither of them had been paid; so, in barbarian terms, they had a great deal to talk about. The conversation went something like this:

"Groan, wass happenin'?"

"Nuffin'. You get paid fer that Legrash job?"

"Nah."

"Me neither."

"See you 'round."

"P'raps."

Gordo was annoyed; he couldn't get a word in edgeways. Instead, he decided to forge a path to the bar. He was halfway through the crowd when a voice rang out over the fray and the entire room fell silent.

EIGHT

YOU COULD have heard a pin drop. Every eye in the house was fixed on the young stranger who had just strode into the center of the room. He stood tall despite his height, and proud, but remained a veritable portrait of curiosity. Chas Firebrand, the tavern owner, leaned forward and put one beer-stained hand to his ear. "Could you repeat that, son?" he said.

"Certainly, humble bartend," Diek spat, an alien energy coursing through his veins. He could feel The Voice welling up inside him. "I wish one of the lesser classes seated in this establishment to announce me at the palace. It won't take very long, and for the privilege, I will spare his life."

On any other day this speech would have been suicide, plain and simple. A knife in the back if Diek were lucky, a knife somewhere else if he weren't. Today was worse. Out of the corner of his eye, Chas noticed that the local thug ring was assembling for a late lunch and, at a corner table, he spotted several likely-looking Yowlers. Chas twitched nervously; it was only a matter of time.

Strangely enough, the boy oozed an ethereal confidence, and several people were edging away from him. One group of thugs, however, was preparing to rise from their seats. They quickly thought better of it when two shapes loomed into view behind the foreigner, one unquestionably dwarfish and the other implausibly muscular.

Diek smiled on, oblivious, as a number of drawn daggers disappeared into pockets and sleeves.

"'Scuse us," said Gordo, shoving his way past. He'd noticed Diek enter the bar and now felt strangely compelled to help him; after all, anyone with no muscles brave enough to talk down to the inhabitants of the Ferret couldn't be far from earning his first million.

He looked up at Diek Wustapha. "I think this, er,

master assassin'll want us to announce him at the palace. Yes?"

The bar, as one, looked momentarily doubtful.

"Um, yes," Diek said, his voice beginning to waver. "You will be adequate, possibly."

"I'd get over to a table pretty sharpish if I were you, lad," Gordo whispered, grabbing Diek's arm. "'Cause talkin' like that in a place like this is gonna get you nailed up real, real quick."

Diek's expression changed to one of confusion. His confidence seemed to desert him and, eyes glazed, he began to sidle toward the nearest vacant table. A number of undesirables made to pursue him, but Groan put a hand to his sword hilt and they quickly reconsidered. Diek reached the table and slumped down onto a stool. His head hurt; it felt as if his mind were involved in a slow and painful wrestling match with some invading army . . . and it was losing. He felt sleep overcome him and realized, for the first time, that he hadn't slept since he'd left Little Irksome.

Slowly, the hubbub of tavern noise rose back to its usual level at the Ferret.

Groan sighed, sniffed, and shoved his way to the bar, Gordo shuffling along in his wake. Most of the conversations had resumed, aside from one being undertaken by a group of zombies in a darkened corner. This was nothing unusual. One of their number had muttered a few syllables just after lunch and was unlikely to complete the sentence by closing time.

"Toofache, please," Groan said, arriving at the bar.

Gordo climbed up onto a stool and gave Chas a sympathetic grin. "It's an old barbarian joke," he said. "Don't for juggers' sake take it the wrong way."

Chas mumbled under his breath and smiled back. "What'll it be, gents?"

"Three, er no, better make that two ales . . . and a peppermint punch," said Gordo. "That kid's going to need a medicinal brew." He rested his battle-axe on the top of a nearby stool. "Groan, you'd better go and see if he's all right. He *is* a foreigner, after all. There might be some money in it."

As the barbarian lurched off in the direction of the table, Gordo turned back to the barman. "How do we get in to see the duke ahead of any competition?" he asked, standing on tiptoe in order to see over the bar.

Chas pointed over toward a table where a figure sat slumped over a mug half filled with ale, the other half having plastered his beard to the table. "See that bloke over there? You could do worse than talk to him. In fact, he might go straight to the palace when he leaves."

"Why, who is he?" asked Gordo, stepping aside as

Groan returned, supporting the foreigner with a ham-size fist gripping his shoulder.

"That's Tambor Forestall, Chairman of the City Council," answered the bartender.

Groan raised the ghost of an eyebrow. "And he drinks in 'ere?"

"Yes."

Gordo frowned. "Doesn't get a lot of attention for being in charge of the council?"

"Nope."

"Why not?" asked Gordo.

"The council don't do naff all in Dullitch. The duke gets blamed for everything."

"Nice," Gordo said, nodding.

"Yeah," Groan agreed. "Seems fair."

Tambor didn't like it when shadows fell across his drinking table, especially during the day. He lowered his head again and tried to examine the bottom of his tankard, but the shadow just kept lengthening.

"Oi, you. Come an' sit wit' us."

Tambor looked up. He soon wished he hadn't. Groan Teethgrit was a sight to behold, but the man was probably not best viewed within the smoky depths of the Ferret. For a moment, Tambor thought he'd become the focus of attention for an angry mountain troll. Then he realized that, against all odds, the creature had spoken syllables, albeit fractured ones. And the face was familiar. Tambor had been an ordinary councillor during the Virgin Sacrifice Scandal, but there were some faces you simply didn't forget.

"I beg your pardon?" Tambor ventured, desperately.

"I said, come an' sit wit' us."

The bulky giant pointed over to a table that was already playing host to a stocky dwarf and a boy who looked severely drugged.

"Um . . . I'm fine as I am, thanks," said Tambor, turning his gaze back to his drink.

"How d'you mean?"

Tambor hesitated. "Er . . . what I mean is, I'd quite like to go on sitting here, if it's all the same to you."

"Right," muttered Groan. "An' I'd like a frog in a box, but we don't always get what we want, do we?"

Tambor managed a weak grin, picked up his drink, and sidled over to the table. The muscled mountain loomed over him.

"Pull up a stool," Gordo said, offering the elderly councillor a companionable smile. "And tell us about this plague of yours."

A sudden, all-knowing look came into Tambor's twinkling eyes. "Ah," he said. "Now I see. You're mercenaries."

"An' you're a damn sorcerer!" boomed Groan, who'd taken offense. "I can spot one a mile off."

The councillor shrugged. "I used to be, back before the art was banned. I was a very good one, too. Not any more, though. Now I'm in politics."

Gordo took a gulp from his tankard, and frowned. "Don't you miss the life of adventure?"

"Desperately . . . but I suppose you can't throw fireballs forever. At least, not in this city. Hahahaha!" Tambor forced a laugh.

"Yeah, so I heard. Any children?" asked Gordo.

"None that'd admit to it. Got a grandson who talks to me, though; young Jimmy. He's a good lad, bit of an idiot, but you know how youngsters are these days. He works down at Spew's, mornings, and scouts for the duke in the afternoons. I think he works at night, too, fetching stuff for people."

"Ah, a noble trade," said Gordo, tactfully.

"All thieves're scum," said Groan, who'd heard of tact but hadn't bought any shares.

"I'll get rid of your plague."

The table fell silent, and three pairs of eyes turned to consider Diek Wustapha. The boy looked momentarily electrified, then slouched forward and collapsed onto the table. Everyone looked at Groan.

"*What?* I didn't touch 'im."

"Kids these days," Tambor mumbled, shaking his head sadly. "Drugged up to the damn eyeballs. Still, this city needs all the help it can get. D'you two think you could help him to the palace?"

Gordo nodded. "I don't know about that," he muttered. "But, if you can get us in, we might be persuaded to dump him inside the door. That way, we get to pitch to the duke, first. Agreed?"

Tambor smiled awkwardly, but the look on Groan's face advised him against argument.

NINE

SLOWLY, Diek returned to consciousness. It was strange waking up in a palace and not remembering how you'd arrived there. It was even stranger waking up dazed and confused in a palace that looked as though it had been designed by a confirmed lunatic. The place was an absolute mess.

Cobwebs parted before Diek as he entered the kitchen. The staff consisted entirely of ghouls, hollow-eyed grave walkers who lurched around without purpose, stopping every few seconds to turn their empty eye sockets toward vats filled with bubbling soup.

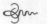

Chickens squawked in cages suspended on ropes from the kitchen ceiling. A dark-skinned wench with a flaking scalp brought down a chopper and severed one of her own fingers, which fell into a bowl of flour. She didn't look too surprised, though; perhaps it was part of the dish. Diek shook his head, wondering if the palace officials ever came down here. He hadn't seen so many dead people walking around since his grandmother's eightieth birthday.

Diek chose the section occupied by the fewest zombies and sidled into it unobtrusively, careful not to draw attention to himself. On reflection, he decided that these people probably wouldn't notice an invasion, and moved on at greater speed.

The central passage wasn't much better. True, it wasn't full of the living dead, but it was full of Modeset family portraits which, though marginally more welcoming, were just as ugly. He fancied that he heard voices echoing far above; so, stepping over a toppled bench, he cautiously ascended the stairs.

A little farther up, he huffed on a pane in an arched landing window, wiped a circle, and peered out. Dullitch sprawled beneath the palace, a cityscape of rooftops and towers. So many people and—he paused to remember the words of the herald—three rats to every man. He had to be confident. *A confident demeanor is second only to a crystal-clear mind, the perfect instrument for attracting faith in others.* The Voice was getting stronger.

Diek shook himself from his reverie; he was beginning to feel unusually disoriented.

"Twice in one day," said Tambor, puffing and panting as he conquered yet another flight of steps. "I'll tell you fellows something for nothing; if I had my time again, I'd choose magic over politics and that's a fact. In my early days, I could've shot up here on a magic carpet."

"You can't go up stairs on a magic carpet," said Pegrand, still straining under his personal burden. "It'd go on a diagonal and you'd fall off."

"Well, I never fell off a magic carpet in ten years as a sorcerer and I'll be damned if I'd have fallen off one going up here."

"It doesn't matter," said Gordo, who'd seen an opening in the conversation. "If you fall off a magic carpet anywhere, you're stuffed. It's always a long way down unless you've just taken off."

"Yeah," said Groan.

Tambor scowled. "Not if you were flying with old Wally Sprinkle. His takeoffs were legendary. Birds used to migrate in accordance with his flight schedules."

"Anyway, we haven't got one now," said Gordo, trying to change the subject.

"Sometimes he didn't even need the carpet," Tambor continued, mumbling to himself. "Just used to take off on his own."

To take his mind off the rat crisis, Duke Modeset had spent the afternoon searching for his current canine companion. He had only seen the dog once since his manservant, Pegrand, had purchased it, and he felt a distant pang of guilt for the neglect.

He was down on his hands and knees, peering into the darkness underneath the ducal throne. From what little he could see, it wasn't a patch on the Snowland husky he used to own, but it was a dog nevertheless, and was probably in need of care and attention. He wondered if it would like a biscuit.

The sound began even before Modeset had attempted to move away. A low-throated snarl rose steadily in pitch and crescendoed to a growl bordering on insanity. Modeset found himself frozen to the spot in sheer terror.

Surely it can't be coming from the dog, he thought, keeping one eye on the curled-up fur ball under the throne. He suddenly realized that he couldn't tell which way the animal was facing. He

was still speculating about it when an eye flicked
open.

Even Diek heard the scream. It ripped through the
palace; ornaments shattered, windows shook, and
latches rattled. He watched as a flock of birds erupted
from the gardens and took flight. Then, just as suddenly, the sound faded away. All was silent.

Diek shook his head. He was beginning to realize
that palaces were very strange places, especially this
one.

Pegrand burst into the throne room and dropped his
pile of luggage. The party of mercenaries and Tambor
Forestall filed in behind him.

"Are you all right, milord?" he said. "Milord . . . ?"

The room appeared entirely empty. Pegrand
looked to the left and right, then up at the ceiling.
Eventually he looked down. "What're you doing on the
floor, milord?" he asked.

Modeset sighed. "Practicing my yoga, Pegrand.
Would you be so kind as to pass me that marrowbone
over by the door?"

The manservant motioned to Tambor, who rushed
over to fetch the bone. He handed it on to Pegrand,
making sure to keep a fair distance between himself

and the shape lurking under the throne. Pegrand tossed it to the dog, then helped the duke to his feet. "That's Vicious," said Pegrand.

"You're telling me," said Modeset.

"No, milord. You named the dog Vicious, remember?"

"Oh, so I did. Quite right, too. Little bast—"

"*These* are the mercenaries, milord," interrupted Pegrand. "You'll, er, you'll probably remember Groan Teethgrit and, um—"

"Yes. Only too well."

In what seemed like the blink of an eye, Modeset crossed the room and seated himself behind his pearly white marble desk. "Assemble!" he shouted.

Pegrand hurried around the room, ushering everyone into a straight line or, at least, the nearest approximation of a straight line they could manage. Groan would've stood out on a map.

"Are these all the mercenaries we have?" Modeset asked.

Tambor thrust one hand into his robe and produced a tattered scrap of parchment. He squinted at it. "There is a young man unconscious downstairs. I believe he is this . . . um . . . how do you say it? I believe it's said Diyek, Diyek Wustaphor," Tambor managed, edging around every vowel as if it might suddenly leap out of the word and bite him.

"I see. Let's just leave him there for the time being, shall we? I'll deal with him later."

Groan muttered under his breath, bumbled across the room, and sat in the throne. Nobody in the room batted an eyelid, but Vicious took the opportunity to gnaw at the barbarian's ankles. It gave up after ten minutes.

Modeset continued: "Now, if we can just—"

"I don't believe you'll have need of these men," said a voice.

Tambor stepped aside to admit the young traveler, who marched over to the desk with an air of authority befitting a king. He treated the duke to a haughty grin.

"My name is Diek Wustapha, and I am the only one who can rid your city of all unwanted guests, for a far lower price than these mercenaries."

Gordo spat on to the mosaic tiles. "How do you know?" he said. "We haven't even quoted a bloody price yet!"

"Don't take it personally, boys!" Tambor shouted. "These yokels, they're all the same."

"My methods will cause little civic unrest," Diek continued. "I'm sure we can come to some arrangement."

His voice had a strange, melodic quality.

Modeset looked from Diek to the mercenaries and

back again. Then he steepled his fingers and used them to prop up his chin. A smile was forming.

Diek strode out of the palace like some sort of dark god, marching with purpose and shoving the occasional surprised maid out of his path. As he arrived at the foot of the central staircase, he snatched a black cloak from an ornate stand and draped it around his shoulders. The sentries, having just signed in for evening duty, parted automatically when he approached, then shuffled back together again like a set of swing doors. No questions were asked when the gates swung open to allow Diek's exit, and no comment was made when they clicked back together behind him.

Tambor Forestall had never been one for company. He'd always preferred spending time by himself. It had nothing to do with the ancient adage about sorcerers being reclusive; he just didn't find people very interesting. Besides, one mercenary tour of the palace a day was enough for him. "Bless the old sprout," that dwarf had muttered under its breath. The nerve of it!

He stared down miserably at his sorcerer's hat, remembering his days of magic. He'd been through some hats in his time. He recalled, many moons ago, the woolen apprentice cap given to him on his arrival at the Velvet Tower in Legrash. He'd then progressed through the ranks of sorcery: from warlock to wizard, mage, and, finally, first-class sorcerer. He still couldn't help but feel, what with all the sniggering and sarcastic remarks over the years, that it hadn't been worth it.

A tickling sensation in his foot made him lean back and peer beneath the tavern table. A small black rat was nibbling at the hole in his boots. He yelped, kicked it away and watched it scurry behind the bar. Then he inspected the boot. It was a pity the city council didn't upgrade boots, he thought to himself. He'd be wearing golden sandals by now.

The Rotting Ferret's special performers for the evening were Farfl, Duk, and Orfo, members of a cross-species band from Legrash. They were currently engaged in a heated dispute with Inky Mamaskin, master hypnotist, who claimed that their performances were sleep inducing and therefore were putting him out of business.

Tambor flicked through a heavy spell book he'd bought from a black-market dealer on Birch Street. Apparently, it was one of the lucky few to escape being burned. He grinned, arriving at a few dusty pages near the back in which he'd already stashed some incidental notes. The volume was in good condition, and practically identical to his original copy; Tambor felt sure the gods had meant for him to find it. "Excuse me?"

A dwarfish face smiled up at him. "Mind if we join you again?" said Gordo, clambering onto a nearby stool without waiting for a reply.

Tambor wondered who the "we" was and looked about him. Where he'd had a clear view of the performance, now there was nothing but solid muscle.

Groan removed his helmet and set it down on the floor beside his stool, disturbing a gang of rats who'd evidently come looking for the one Tambor had booted behind the bar.

"What's happening tonight, then?" said Gordo. "Enjoying yourself?"

"Not much," said Tambor. "Getting old isn't all it's cracked up to be."

He turned his empty mug upside down on the table and belched.

Gordo shook his head, sadly. "We've just traveled over land and, er, grass to save this city from a major"—he paused—"ratastrophe." He nudged Groan in the elbow but got no reaction. "And, d'you know what happened? Of course you do—the duke gave the job to a damn shepherd!"

"Doesn't surprise me a bit," said Tambor, ignoring the accusation and staring gloomily at his upturned mug. "City's run by ne'er-do-wells and bad politicians."

"You're both, ain't you?" said Groan.

The sorcerer smirked humorlessly. "One or the other. In practice it amounts to the same thing. One big chain. Oh sure, there's the council, but the city pretty much runs itself without too much hindrance from anyone but the duke."

"Who's that li'l fella over there?" said Tambor, pointing toward a corner table at the back of the room. "He's smaller than you!" he said, nodding his head at the dwarf.

Gordo tried to see where the old sorcerer was looking, in case there was a relative he could sit with. His gaze fell on a bright red hat with green flowers painted on it. "That's a gnome, you silly old fool."

Tambor blinked. "Ah," he said. "What's the difference?"

"Dwarfs is bigger," said Groan, to show he was paying attention. "An' dwarfs 'as got beards, an' dwarfs is fatter, an—"

"All right!" Gordo snapped. "I think he's got the point."

"Why's he just sittin' there, then?" asked Groan.

Tambor coughed over his beer mug and gave himself a froth moustache on top of his beard. "P'raps he's got gnome to go to," he said, and spent the next minute in quiet hysterics.

"May the gods help us," said Gordo, looking out at the encroaching darkness. "Look, we'd better start thinking about lodgings. We can't stay here all night, and I'll be damned if I'm going back home without a brass nickel. The village elders would have me in disgrace."

"Stay 'ere with me," said Tambor, throwing one arm around Gordo and making a valiant attempt to get the other midway round Groan. "My grandson's comin' to meet me in a minute. He's a semi prof—proffec—proffectional thief. Gonna work for the Yowlers, he is. Best in the city."

"Marvelous," said Gordo.

TEN

JIMMY QUICKSTINT was the most incompetent thief in the history of organized crime. The chandelier creaked as he swung back and forth.

Jimmy looked up at the chandelier—just as the chain snapped.

It wasn't a great fall, but it was certainly an unfortunate one. Most of the room was carpeted but, as fate would have it, Jimmy landed heavily on a square of floor Lord Moffet had purposely overlooked when the money ran out. The chandelier landed on top of him. I should've been a beggar, Jimmy thought.

He heard someone approaching and, straining to lift his head, he turned to see who it was. A hairy Alsatian trotted over to him. And lifted one leg.

"Where's that no-good grandson of mine?" said Tambor, who had passed through two giggling fits and was nearing genuine joviality.

Chas Firebrand leaned over his shoulder and collected three empty mugs. He then wiped each one "clean" with the flap of his beer-stained apron and passed them to the barmaid, a pretty young lass who had just fluttered in and caused Groan to pass out.

"What's he look like, this boy of yours?" said Gordo, checking Groan's pulse to make sure his friend was still breathing.

"Silly young bugger," said Tambor. "Got his father's face and his mother's walk—or is it the other way round . . . ?"

Chas frowned at the barbarian. "Dear oh dear," he said, shaking his head. "He all right, is he?"

"He shouldn't drink so much; it's obviously bad for him."

"No it isn't," said Tambor, reprehensively. "I look after my drink, I do. Take it home with me."

Chas winced. "Blimey," he said. "That's some capacity you've got there, old man."

Tambor smiled at the middle distance, then tried and failed to get up.

Halfway along Tanner Avenue, Jimmy Quickstint stopped and kicked out at the nearest wall in frustration. Then he unfolded the night's remaining assignment and read:

Date: Thursday 43rd Fortune, 1002
Assignment Location: 14 Sack Avenue
Task: Golden serpent shaped idol
Objective: Retrieval
PLEASE INCINERATE AFTER DIGESTION

Jimmy had always wondered if the last bit was metaphorical. Did they really expect you to eat it first, then set light to it? Even the Yowler's multi-stomached mutant members would have had their work cut out trying that. He read the note through twice before producing a tinderbox from his knee pocket and igniting the paper. Sack Avenue, eh? The Rich District, the Merchants' Quarter. He smiled to himself. This was it, his last chance to make it big. He would pass this assignment with flying colors and become Jimmy Quickstint, first-grade Yowler thief. Well, not quite. He still had to perform some exclusive,

never-to-be-repeated act of theft for his coursework,
but an honors entry to the Runners proper did not
come easy. You'd have to steal something truly amazing to pull that one off.

He replaced the tinderbox and headed in the
direction of Sack Avenue.

Several streets away, Diek Wustapha was heading
toward the decrepit mouth of Dullitch's ancient sewer
system. Footsteps clicking on the cobbles, he made his
approach. Surprising himself, he raised a pointed finger toward the moss-covered doors of the sewer, and
watched in amazement as a plume of green flame burst
forth and burned the lichen away. As the flames died
down, Diek's other hand shot up and the sewer doors
flew outward and crashed to the ground.

Diek searched for his flute and automatically
brought the instrument to his lips: he could already
hear the rats approaching.

Groan had recovered from his fainting episode with
alarming speed. He was now over at the bar chatting
away to the barmaid, who smiled coquettishly and
chuckled on cue. As Gordo watched, he reflected that,
when it came to women, Groan was never slow on the
uptake.

Tambor, on the other hand, was out for the count. It was way past the old man's bedtime, and his head rested face-first in a plate of prunes he had only got a quarter of the way through.

"Like her," said Groan, returning to his seat with two giant mugs of something frothy. He banged one down in front of Gordo. "She said we could 'ave these on the 'ouse."

The dwarf peered inside his mug, suspiciously. "What's that red thing floating in there?" he asked.

"Hem'rhoid, I fink," said Groan. "She said her farver's bought himself a cherry orchard, on account of his trouble."

Gordo took the statement on board but decided it was best left unraveled.

"Can I help you, sir?"

The voice shattered the silky silence of the night and Jimmy froze. Absolute terror descended on him like a sackful of lead. He spun around to find a member of the City Guard, a wiry man of no height with a bulbous nose, looking up at him quizzically.

"No, thank you," Jimmy replied, tapping his foot on the ground in what he hoped was a nonchalant, carefree manner.

"It's just that, well, I can't help noticin' that you

seem to be actin' somewhat suspiciously," said the guard, eyeing the boy inquisitively.

"Ah, I see. Er—"

"Are you a Yowler by any chance?"

"What, me? No, sir! What an idea!"

"Hmm . . . well, if you're not robbing the house, then what, may I ask, are you doing in the front garden?"

Jimmy's mind raced frantically for a plausible explanation. Unfortunately, none came to him. "I'm the gardener," he said, unable to think of anything more likely.

The guard continued to stare up at him, now sporting a look of vague incomprehension. "Funny time to be gardening, isn't it? I mean, I've heard of—"

"I'm trying to find a special flower for his Lordship's indoor collection," interrupted Jimmy, who was now talking too fast to think.

"Why can't you do that in the mornin'?" asked the guard.

"Because it's a special flower that only comes out at night."

Strangely, this last explanation seemed to appear distantly plausible to the guard and he looked momentarily baffled. "A nocturnal plant? Are you puttin' me on?"

"No, it's true," said Jimmy, beginning to believe his own story. "Usually they appear only in the Gleaming Mountains; 'phodo' they're called. 'Phodosithnisses.'"

"Fair enough," the guard nodded and turned to leave. "Sorry to have bothered you."

He stopped halfway toward the elderly wooden gateposts and turned around, a tired smile playing on his lips. He seemed to study the authenticity of Jimmy's ludicrous facial expression, before whistling in an awkward fashion and disappearing into the gathering evening mist. Jimmy sighed with relief and prepared himself for the climb. The only foothold attainable from a standing position came in the form of one of the hinges that attached the drainpipe to the brickwork. He thrust his right foot hard between wall and iron and pulled himself toward his goal. . . .

He'd nearly reached the first-floor window when he slipped.

Jimmy scrambled frantically, his feet beating against the brickwork in a valiant attempt to relieve the pressure on his aching arms. Finally he managed to regain his grip, haul himself through the narrow window, and slither into the room beyond.

Relief swept over him.

Jimmy made a number of keen observations about the candlelit chamber he now occupied. The first was that the golden idol he was looking for rested on a cushion inside an ornate glass cabinet standing against the east wall. Then, in the following order, he noticed the lock on the cabinet door; the imposing four-poster bed with an elderly couple snoring away peacefully inside it; and, finally, the key fastened on the chain hanging around the sleeping old man's neck. In the silent shadows of that room, Jimmy discovered why the Rooftop Runners had just thirty-seven members. This situation looked, to all intents and purposes, impossible. How on earth was he supposed to retrieve the cursed key without waking the old boy?

Suddenly the figure lying next to the key holder shifted uncomfortably beneath the blankets. Jimmy looked on in fascinated horror as the old woman sat up, swung her legs over the side of the bed, and shuffled into a pair of bedroom slippers. Lord Buckly stirred in his sleep as his wife disturbed a number of creaking floorboards on her way to the door. Jimmy remained still, a silhouette against the window. When the old woman had departed, he breathed a sigh of relief; perhaps luck favored him tonight, after all. It was as he considered his good fortune that a plan became clear to him. He crept forward, dodging the planks that the old woman had identified on her noisy journey a few moments before.

Hesitating to consider the implications should his plan fail, Jimmy climbed into the rickety four-poster bed and pulled the covers up over him. He remained perfectly still for a few seconds, pondering on how to advance his movement. Then, with lightning dexterity, he shot out a hand and looped the key up and over the old man's head in one swift movement. Even Uole Twonk (the greatest thief in Dullitch history) would have been proud.

The key now in his possession, Jimmy lay panting on the bed with the satisfaction of success. He was about to climb out when a hand reached around his waist and grasped him tightly. At first he feared that Buckly had awakened, but then it became apparent that the old lord, though sleeping, simply desired some affection from his wife. The thief considered briefly what her Ladyship would do in this situation and con sequently shoved the old man aside.

The key turned in the lock with a loud click, and Jimmy snatched up the idol, which felt strangely sticky against his palm. Reaching down into his trousers, he pulled out the sack and tried, in vain, to slip the ornament inside. It wouldn't leave his hand. The vindictive old fool had daubed the piece with glue!

However, Jimmy had no time to revise his actions, as Lady Buckly was now on her way back up the stairs, footsteps echoing loudly through the open door. Jimmy considered his drastic situation and dashed toward the window. He burst from the first floor of 14 Sack Avenue in a shower of glass and landed awkwardly in the petunia patch he had managed to avoid earlier. As screams erupted from the room above and various lights flicked on all over the Merchants' Quarter, Jimmy struggled to his feet and frantically kicked over a group of dustbins.

Unfortunately he didn't have time to snatch up the idol—which had fallen off, along with half the skin from the palm of his hand—before Lord Buckly's thirteen hounds bore down on him.

"We can't leave until his grandson turns up," said Gordo, indicating the unconscious Tambor with a nod of his head.

Groan looked puzzled. "Why not?" he asked.

"Because," Gordo began, wondering about his own chances with the barmaid. "Well, it just wouldn't be right, that's all."

The barbarian sniffed and downed his ale.

High above the streets of Dullitch, a shadow danced along the rooftops.

Jimmy dropped down a level, walked a little way with his back pressed firmly against a wall, and arrived at the ledge edge of City Hall. Problem. There was a considerable space between the roof of the building and the roof of the Alchemist Museum.

He slid down a slated section of roof and onto a lower ledge, feeling the first touch of rain on his cheek. His fingers, which had been groping frantically at the wall in case he lost his footing, found glass. He turned and peered through the window into a well-furnished office. He wondered how hard it would be to shatter the largest pane: too hard, probably.

Far below in the street, a figure ascended the large flight of stairs that led to City Hall. A door opened and closed again. Jimmy didn't pay much attention.

As he was looking into the room, two things happened in quick succession. First the light came on and then somebody opened the window. Outward.

"Oi," said Groan, nudging Gordo's helmet with his elbow. "You 'member that 'erald what met us on the road? He's jus' walked in."

Jimmy had entered the Ferret and was in the process of apologizing to all and sundry as he bumped his way to the bar. He was covered in hay. Gordo watched as he stumbled up to Chas Firebrand and muttered something in his ear. Then he looked over in their direction and sauntered toward the table.

"That's my granddad," Jimmy said, pointing at the unconscious councillor and smiling feebly.

"Aye," said Gordo.

"Wanna make somefink out of it?" said Groan, who immediately took issue with anyone who began his sentences with claims of ownership.

"Nice helmet," said Jimmy conversationally, nodding down at the battered-looking piece of metal by Gordo's feet. "Mind if I join you?"

"Sure," said Gordo. "Did you have a nice walk back?"

"Eh? Oh, yeah, thanks for that."

The dwarf grinned. "Sorry. No hard feelings. I'm afraid yer' granddad here's the worse for drink."

"He's sleepin'," translated Groan with satisfaction.

Gordo belched. "Why are you all covered in that stuff?"

"Accident," said Jimmy, smiling. "Thank the gods for hay carts, that's what I say."

"Hmm . . . You know where we can get lodgings at this hour?" asked Gordo.

"Well, there's always Finlayzzon's," said Jimmy. "Or, at a push, I s'pose I could sneak you into one of the Yowler hideouts." He looked wretched at the thought of *that*.

"No," said Gordo. "That first place you mentioned should be okay. Where is it?"

"On Stainer Street. 'S not far." He sniffed and scratched his chin. "Only, I wondered—"

"Yes?"

"Well—"

"What is it?" snapped Gordo impatiently.

"I don't suppose you could take Granddad with you?" He snatched one of Tambor's prunes and popped it into his mouth. "Only, his landlady's a right old dragon and she's threatened to kick him out if he comes home in the small hours again."

"What?" Gordo exclaimed. "But he's the council chairman, isn't he? Are you seriously telling me he hasn't even got his own house?"

Jimmy gave the dwarf a nervous grin. "Politics doesn't pay you much of a wage in Dullitch," he whispered.

ELEVEN

IT WAS MORNING in Dullitch, and a cool breeze bothered a dragon-shaped weathervane on the roof of the treasury. It spun around, whistled on the wind, and broke off, embedding itself point down in the sloping lower roof. A chimney sweep, who had narrowly averted being impaled by leaping out of its path, fell six floors and crashed through a striped canopy over Stovers' pie shop.

Duke Modeset smiled bitterly and turned away from the window. "I hate this city, Pegrand," he said. "Well, maybe that's an overstatement, but I'm sure there are better places to rule. Anthills, for example."

"Ha! I don't care for it much myself, milord," said Pegrand. "I saw three trolls out on Banana Bridge yesterday, dangling a young lad and his mum over the side. It oughtn't to be allowed. It's not just thieves these days, milord. Most of our citizens are petty crooks and vagabonds, too."

And worse, he thought. I'm not going to mention that dwarf with the butcher's daughter. He'd never seen such despicable behavior.

"Just concentrate on the job *you're* doing, Pegrand."

"I am, milord," said the manservant. "But you did say normal duties were on hold until—"

"Exactly! So, you see, in some ways you can actually think of this rat crisis as an *extended* vacation, albeit one taken at home."

"How's that, milord?" Pegrand raised an eyebrow. There had definitely been an emphasis on the word *extended*, and he wasn't sure he liked the implication. "Surely you're not actually thinking of staying here during the attempted, er, rat-out, milord?" he said, his voice edged with despair. "Do you remember that idea you had a few months ago of faking your own death? Maybe you should try that now!"

"What?"

"Well, maybe this infestation is a blessing in

disguise; an opportunity to leave this fleapit of a city to someone else. It's a terrible place, milord."

"As we both agree," said Duke Modeset. "But I'm sure I don't know why *you* continue to live here."

Modeset got down on his hands and knees and peered under the throne. Vicious was still curled up in a ball, growling softly in its sleep. He wondered what sex the dog was.

"Um . . . excuse me, gentlemen?"

Modeset and Pegrand started. The lord chancellor, a thin and insipid man named Quarry, stood beside the throne. He was attempting to shuffle through a collection of scrolls while standing up. Every few seconds a rogue parchment would slide off and drift away.

"I was thinking about the money situation, Duke Modeset," said Quarry.

"Oh, yes?" answered the duke.

"Indeed," said Quarry.

Pegrand sniffed haughtily and marched over to the window. He'd always despised chancellors, but Quarry was definitely a snake in the grass if ever he'd seen one.

"Problems?" asked the duke.

"Well," Chancellor Quarry continued, "we've been experiencing some financial difficulties since the citizens stopped paying their taxes."

Duke Modeset's eyes narrowed. "When was that?"

"About a year ago, sir. The shopkeepers still pay theirs and all small businesses are assessed a fixed sum per annum, but we've built up a backlog of debt with Legrash, you see, and—"

"Tell me, Quarry," Duke Modeset asked, approaching the question with caution. "Exactly what do we have in the treasury, at this precise moment?"

The chancellor hurried over to the desk, snatched up a quill and did some rudimentary calculations. "About—"

"Yes?" said Modeset, his eyebrows raised.

"Roughly—"

"Mmm?"

"Seven hundred and fifty-seven thousand, five hundred and twelve . . ."

Pegrand breathed a sigh of relief, and even Modeset's death-mask features expressed a second or two of surprised satisfaction.

". . . sacks of Coral's cut-price coal," the chancellor continued, smiling weakly. "A present from Baron Quaker of Legrash," he added.

"Coal. I see," said the duke calmly, his death mask returning.

"Coal?" echoed Pegrand. "I suggest we hang this man, milord."

"Silence, Pegrand! We'll do nothing of the sort."

The chancellor exhaled.

"We'll let him explain it to the young man when he comes asking for his reward," said Modeset. He smiled at Quarry. "I'm sure it's the very least you can do."

"Certainly, Duke Modeset. It would be a pleasure."

After all, Quarry thought, he's only a country-sider. What can *he* do?

Diek stood on the crest of the tor and stared down at Dullitch, sprawled across the landscape. It projected onto the Nasbeck Ocean like a dirty brown smudge. *This is all just scenery, the crusty flesh covering an underworld of creeping darkness. We are here, Diek. We are . . . waiting for you. But first you must rid these people of their plague . . . of their . . . burden. Do it, Diek. Now, now is your time. And so it shall be. Play, Diek. PLAY. . . .*

He froze; The Voice was worrying him now. He raised a hand to his head, fearful that the tide of his own mind was about to turn on him again. . . .

Gordo had woken up in a few hellholes during his time, but he had to admit Finlayzzon's took some beating. It was more a jail than a boardinghouse. Godrick Finlayzzon was a wealthy entrepreneur who had risen in status by thinking several steps ahead of his rivals and planning carefully for any anticipated complications. A grimy notice warned that guests would be locked in their rooms until they'd paid for the accommodation. In typical Dullitch style, the note was nailed to the *back* of the door.

"Can't you pay him?" Tambor snapped.

"Listen, you ungrateful chump," said Gordo. "Your bungling dunce of a grandson got us all into this mess in the first place, so *you* can get us out."

"But I haven't got any money!"

"Can't you conjure it open?" snapped Gordo.

"What, the door?" asked Tambor.

"Yes, the door! Better still, *order* it open; you're head of the bleedin' council, aren't you?"

"Not anymore," Tambor murmured. "I'm deserting."

"You're what?" gasped Gordo.

"You've inspired me! I'm deserting the council for a life of magic and high adventure!"

"And yet you can't open a single damn door?"

"Nope; I, well, I left my spell book at the Ferret," answered Tambor quietly.

"And you can't perform a simple lock-picking without it? Some sorcerer you are."

The dwarf stamped over to the window. Bars. You

had to take your hat off to this Finlayzzon, he'd really thought of everything. Besides, it was quite a jump.

"Can't your barbarian wrench the door off?" asked Tambor.

Gordo treated Groan to a doubtful look. "Can you?"

Groan marched purposefully over to the door and gave it a determined test kick. Some plaster cracked on the walls. "Should fink so," he said. "Stan' back."

Tambor had never seen a kick like it. Even Gordo gasped. The door flew out of the wall, taking the entire frame with it. Groan walked out into the hallway as if he were taking a morning stroll through the park. Gordo picked up his axe and beckoned to the old sorcerer, noticing how unstable the ceiling was beginning to look. Hairline cracks and patchwork crumbles sprouted along the east wall, and the window had dropped out, bars and all. The trio threaded their way along the corridor and down the stairs. Tambor made to leave a tip in the boardinghouse's Voluntary Contribution Box, remembered he didn't have any money, and stole a handful of loose change instead.

"Where're we off to now?" he called, hurrying across the cobbles to catch up with Gordo, who in turn was waddling quickly in order to keep pace with Groan.

"We?" Gordo snapped. "What do you mean 'we'? There is no *we*. There's only *us*."

Tambor tripped over the scraggly ends of his robe and snatched at the dwarf's shoulder in an effort to regain his balance. "Hey, I told you, I'm going back to a life of high adventure. I'm going to be a renegade sorcerer!"

"Yeah. So?" said Gordo, still scurrying to keep up with Groan.

"So, I'm exactly what you need to complete your band."

"We're not startin' a band," Groan mumbled. "We're mercen'ries."

"Yes, well, you know what I mean."

"Besides, I 'ate sorc'ry," continued Groan.

"Ha! That's because you don't understand it."

"All right, then," Groan boomed. "We're 'eadin' up to Phlegm, see if there's any o' them merchant caravans we can raid. You can come wiv us, 'f you want."

Gordo stopped dead, and Tambor practically walked over him. Groan marched on a few yards, found he was talking to himself, and mooched back. "What's up wiv you?" he said, looking down at the dwarf but avoiding eye contact.

"He's in?" Gordo exclaimed. "Just like that? What happened to the Groan Teethgrit who won't have anything to do with sorcery?"

"I just fort it might be good to have him wiv' us, is all. In case we ever need a sorc'rer."

"Thanks," said Tambor, weakly.

"Are you serious? He can't even open a damn door!" cried Gordo.

"That's not fair! I told you, I left my spell book in the Ferret," whined Tambor.

"Well, you'd better go and get it, then," snapped Gordo. "You're certainly no use to us without it."

"Fine," said Tambor, glaring back at both of them. "I'll pick up my magic carpet as well. Are you coming?"

"Nah," said Groan. "Meet us at the gates in an hour."

In the Ferret, Jimmy Quickstint concentrated, fanned out his hand, and flipped over the top card of the deck. "Slipper!" said Jimmy, grinning down at his card.

"That's never slipper!" shouted Chas Firebrand. "You need a five or a twelve for slipper. You've only got three sevens."

He snatched up the pack, shuffled and dealt again. "I'm not letting you have another one on 'I owe you,'" he added. "That's more 'n twenty crowns you owe me already."

"No, I can't owe that much," Jimmy protested.

"You do. Remember that stunt at closing time, last week?"

Jimmy tried to fake confusion. "Er, don't recall exactly—"

"I bet you don't, my foot," said Chas moodily, cracking his knuckles.

"Okay, okay, don't get miffed," said Jimmy. He slipped off his stool, collected a handful of mugs from the nearest table, and placed them behind the bar. "There you go," he added. "Don't say I never do anything for you."

Chas shook his head in disbelief and downed the remnants of his own ale. "You know your problem?" he said.

"No. What?"

"You've got no sense of responsibility. I'm right, aren't I?"

"Could be, could be," answered Jimmy.

"Take your granddad, last night. There he was, passed out over the table, and who had to see that he got a decent night's sleep? Two complete strangers. You didn't know them from Morris. They could've taken him into an alley and beaten him senseless. I bet you haven't even checked to see if he's all right. Your own family. It's unthinkable."

Jimmy closed one eye and cocked his head. "He's an

ex-sorcerer," he said. "He can take care of himself."

"Yeah? So what's he gonna do, pull a rabbit out of a hat and hope it gives one of 'em a nasty bite? Oh, and by the way, he left this here last night. If the rest of the council find out about it, he'll be thrown outta the city."

Chas reached under the bar and produced a grubby, moth-eaten tome. The once-gold lettering was faded, but Jimmy could just make out the word *Grimoire*. "That can't be good," he admitted. "I don't think Granddad knows that many spells as it is. Give it here."

Jimmy stowed the book inside his jerkin, and without another word, hurried out of the tavern.

"Oi! What about my twenty crowns?" shouted Chas, shaking his head in disapproval and pulling himself a pint. He was on his third gulp when Tambor appeared, puffing and panting, in the doorway.

"Chas, are you? All right? Is it? Spell book. Left it, need it. Can I? Have?" Tambor clutched at his chest, struggling to catch his breath.

"You're about five minutes too late," Chas said, downing the rest of his pint. "Jimmy's got it. He's out there looking for you, now."

"Of all the *flkfjjdjs*!"

"Cor blimey, is that Orcish?" asked Chas.

"No, it's modern obscenity." Tambor aimed a kick at the door, and missed. Then he turned and headed out onto the street. "Tell Jimmy I'm leaving Dullitch," he called back.

"You what?" Chas yelled. "Since when?"

"This morning! I'm joining a band of bloodthirsty mercenaries. To hell with you all! *Hahahahahaha!*"

Elsewhere in the city trouble was brewing. . . .

It began as the merest hint of a tremor, a ripple in the water bowl of audibility. Some dust drifted between ceiling and floor in a cellar beneath the Ackerman Fishery. Vicious pricked up half an ear. The sound was distant, almost lost on the wind. It teetered on the brink of existence . . . and began to rise.

Rumble.

"Pegrand?"

Rumble.

"Milord?"

Rumble.

"Is that your stomach?"

Rumble.

"No, milord. I thought it might be yours."

Crash.

Outside, atop the Crest Hill, Diek Wustapha played his terrible melody, while far above him lightning cast a net of electric veins across the sky. For the few folk abroad on the streets lucky or, depending on your view, *unlucky* enough to witness the music, its tune shifted in and out of audibility, high and low, thunderous and harmonious. For the briefest of moments, the townspeople were captivated. However, the real captives were the rising, swelling waves of rats that appeared from the basements and the gutters, knitting together and tumbling toward the lure.

A door burst open somewhere in the southern half of the city. A woman screamed. Nothing happened for a whole minute. Then she was joined by others. Windows were flung open. People rushed out into the streets. A few of the braver citizens were attempting to get a good view of the episode by climbing out onto the rooftops and negotiating precarious slopes filled with damaged slates. Everyone wanted to see what was causing the uproar.

Diek Wustapha was strolling calmly through the streets, a merry melody rising from the flute he raced back and forth between his lips. He had a miniature city-issue map in one hand and stopped at various junctions, regarding it critically.

A rat emerged from the open cellar of a tavern on Stainer Street as the Bakeman's Brewery cart unloaded a barrel of ale. It was followed by others, a dozen, a score, and a hundred or more. Then a multitude, a million, a mischief.

They swarmed between the houses, piling over one another to reach the magical music. Some were as tiny as mice, some were as large as kittens. Some were cute and cuddly, some were disfigured monstrosities. They needed the melody, yearned to reach it, scurrying faster and faster past streets whose inhabitants stood frozen in their wake. On and on they went, scrabbling with greater urgency at every turn.

"Will you look at that!" Chas Firebrand spat, leaning against the door of the Ferret. "He's taking the rats! Unbelievable! Criminals in this city, they'll steal anything!"

He saw a flurry erupting from his own cellar. "Oi!" he shouted, to no one in particular. "I want a crown each for those!"

"Hey," called a passing beggar. "Are you insane? He's doing us all a favor."

"Hah! Not me, I likes rats, I do."

The beggar shook his head in amazement. "Yeah, well," he muttered. "There's always one, isn't there?"

At the mouth of an alley just off the corner of Stainer Street and the Goodwalk, Malcolm Siddle stood on the back of the Grim Company cart and stared in amazement as the sea of vermin swept past.

"Hey, Mr. Grim!" he shouted. "What d'ya think of all this?"

His superior watched as the last of the seething horde rounded Stainer Street. "Well, that's us out of a job," he said.

The gates of the city slammed shut and there came a resounding hum. Then there was nothing but ear-splitting silence.

"I hope we have all learned a valuable lesson from this," said Duke Modeset, from the battlements of Dullitch Palace. "If you want a job done properly, always go out into the countryside and find a simpleton to do it for you."

Pegrand and Chancellor Quarry nodded.

"I think that's the last we're likely to see of our furry friends," the duke continued. "But not, I expect, the last we've seen of the great Wustapha. He, of course, will be coming for his money."

Pegrand sneered and sidled away. Modeset turned to face the chancellor and smiled humorlessly.

"I told the young man he could collect his reward from the treasury, Mr. Quarry. I trust you've thought of a believable excuse?"

He got no reply.

TWELVE

 S IX MILES out from Dullitch, Diek Wustapha stood on a narrow wooden jetty that extended into the Winter River and watched the first of the rats plummet to their doom. A few cunning exceptions managed to shake off the hypnotic melody long enough to swim for the shore, but a terrible, unseen force pushed them back until they too sank beneath the surface of the water. Diek felt no sorrow for them; in fact, he was moving like a puppet, watching himself from outside his own mind like some sort of unwelcome visitor. The

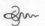

Voice was taking over. Occasionally, it would leave him for an hour or so, as if off on some errand or reporting back to some invisible master, yet it would always return, more powerful and somehow more irresistible than it had been before. . . .

As for the tune he was playing or where it came from, he had little notion. Indeed, he couldn't even remember consciously making a decision to offer his services. It had just sort of happened. Come to think of it, he was only dimly aware of having left for Dullitch in the first place. The whole episode was like some strange dream, complete in every detail without need of his mental application. He was experiencing an icy calm. The voices had gone.

The rats continued to roll over one another, careering toward the icy embrace of oblivion.

Far off to the west, a storm was brewing. Gray clouds gathered over the Varick Pass. Diek shivered and pulled his cloak tight around him. Then he looked back in the direction of Dullitch, where the sun was disappearing between clouds heavy with rain. It was one of those days that just couldn't make up its mind.

"I was thinking," said Duke Modeset, "about something along the lines of 'finders keepers, losers never stray.'"

"I think you've got a bit mixed up there, milord," said Pegrand thoughtfully.

"Well, whatever, it's the principle of the thing. He bails out when the fire gets hot, I don't see why I should burn down my own kitchen." Modeset blinked. That definitely didn't sound right.

"Are we still talking about the foreigner, milord?"

"No, no, no! I'm talking about the chef. I fired him this morning. He's the worst one we've had yet, him and those wretched zombies he has working for him. It's like a morgue in that kitchen. The gods only know what drops off them when they're cooking."

"Er, yes, I see, milord. If I might change the subject, we haven't heard anything from young Wustapha yet."

"And?"

"Well, I just wonder what he's done with all those rats."

"Who cares?" said the duke, dismissively. "As long as they are out of Dullitch, they're somebody else's concern."

"Let's just hope he's not taken them to Legrash, milord. Otherwise we might have to give back some of that coal."

Modeset smiled. "Dear, dear friend," he said. "Always the thinker, eh?"

"Whenever I'm given the initiative, milord."

The duke regarded his manservant out of the corner of one eye. "Was that sarcasm, Pegrand?"

"No, milord. Absolutely not: I wouldn't dream of it."

Duke Modeset nodded. "Good man."

The following morning, there came a thunderous knocking on the doors of the treasury. A panel slid open.

"Yeah?"

Diek stared at a face. It wasn't a particularly nice face. In fact, it only qualified for membership within society because it had all the correct bits. Diek couldn't even put a race to it. "My name is Diek Wustapha," he said, authoritatively. "I have come for my reward."

"Hold on," said the face and disappeared into the shadows.

After a minute or so, it returned. "No can do," it said. "My orders say you've got to go see the chancellor."

"Is that right? And where would I find him?"

The panel slid shut, and there was some whispering. Then it shot open again. "Follow the alley round to the back of the Treasury. There you'll find a small door with a gold plate next to it. Knock three times for the chancellor's secretary."

Diek waited for a time, expressionless. Then he turned and walked around to the alley.

The chancellor's secretary was a man of few words, and he looked positively resentful even to let those go.

"Sit." he snapped, having directed Diek into the sitting area. "Wait."

Just over an hour later, Diek was admitted to the chancellor's inner sanctum.

Quarry was seated behind his desk, both hands flat on the tabletop and a faint smile playing on his lips. "Welcome, Mr. Wustapha," he said. "Any problems?"

"None whatsoever," answered Diek, his eyes narrowing to slits. "I understood that I was to collect my payment from the Treasury. When I arrived there, I was told you wished to see me beforehand. So I'll ask you the same question you just asked me: are there any problems, chancellor?"

There was something in the boy's voice that Quarry was quite certain he didn't like one little bit. It had undertones in it. He was sure countrysiders shouldn't have voices with undertones.

"As a matter of fact, Mr. Wustapha," he said, "there are."

"Oh?"

"Before I go into all that," Quarry went on. "I must ask you: what did you do with the rats?" He crossed his fingers under the table, for luck.

"I drowned them," said Diek, a sudden flash of mock concern showing on his face. "You didn't want them back, did you?"

Quarry's grin could have melted lead. "No no, of course not," he answered. "We just wanted to be certain that our plague would not return to, well, plague us."

"There's little chance of that," Diek said, with rancor. "Now, where are my thousand crowns?"

Quarry's eyes widened. "Goodness gracious," he exclaimed. "Is that what the good duke told you? A thousand crowns? For sweeping out a few rats?"

Diek's face remained expressionless, but deep inside his mind, The Voice was becoming razor edged: he could feel it, once again, starting to take over.

"Is that your final word, chancellor?" asked Diek, his voice suddenly shifting to an icy, inhuman tone.

"I, um, beg your pardon?" stammered Quarry.

"You have no intention of paying me what I'm owed? Is that your final word?"

Quarry started. He was beginning to get the feeling that he'd missed the middle of the conversation. His fears weren't calmed by Diek's sudden smile or by the icy glaze over his eyes.

"I'm sorry," Quarry managed. The room became silent, a dark, brooding quiet that was more unsettling than a hundred heated disputes. Quarry felt something else was required from him. "We simply haven't the funds to pay you," he added.

"And you knew this when you set me to the task?" continued Diek.

"Yes."

"I see. Thank you, Chancellor Quarry."

Diek said nothing more. He simply rose from his seat, opened the door and strode out into the hallway. The portal closed with a decisive click.

"What do you mean 'gone'?" said Jimmy Quickstint.

"All three of 'em together," said Finlayzzon, "just before the rats left. They wrecked the joint on their way out, I might add. *And they robbed my donation box*; how low can you sink, eh?"

He waited to see if there was any emotional reaction from the lad. "Well?"

"Well what?" said Jimmy. "You don't expect *me* to pay for them, surely?"

Finlayzzon shrugged. "You said you were a relative."

"Yeah, I am," said Jimmy. "The poor relation."

"Ah . . . pity."

"Yes, it is. Now, do you have any idea where they went?"

Finlayzzon shook his head.

"Thanks," said Jimmy. "I'll make sure to point all my friends away from here in the future."

"Good!" Finalyzzon called after him. "At least it'll keep the thieves out."

Diek stumbled through the streets, his head swimming with rage and confusion. The crowds swarmed around him. So much noise and so many people. *But you know another tune, don't you, Diek?* He stopped, looked around, and grabbed the arm of a passing juggler.

"What did you say?" he asked.

The man looked bewildered, shook himself free. "Here," he said. "What's your problem, mate?"

Diek shook his head.

"You're nuts, you are," said the juggler, taking a few steps back and colliding with an old woman selling herbal remedies.

You know another tune, Diek.

"Shut up!"

And a place, a magical limbo for traitors.

"Stop! Go away!" shouted Diek, clasping the sides of his head.

THIRTEEN

N IGHT ARRIVED in Dullitch unfathomably fast.

A single light flickered in the topmost tower of Dullitch Palace. Duke Modeset was scribbling. It was something he'd done ever since he was a boy, whenever he'd had trouble sleeping. He'd take a quill and a clean scrap of parchment and scratch down all his thoughts; get them out into the open, as it were. Then he'd take them along to a telepathic in town where the underlying message would be unraveled. Usually it was something like,

You need more greens or a prune or two in the morning to keep your bowels open.

Modeset put down the quill and started; he'd drawn a rat. This was turning into quite a fixation. It was the same reason he'd had trouble sleeping, visited in the small hours by nightmare scenarios that had him sprinting across desert wastelands, pursued by seething hordes of rodent marauders. And Diek Wustapha. The countrysider had been out in front, producing terrible melodies without need of any kind of instrument. They just sort of emanated from him, as if he had a gland for producing music.

Modeset shivered. This was ridiculous. Besides, he'd come to a decision: it was time to abdicate. As soon as the war with Phlegm was won, assuming it *could* be won (assuming, in fact, that anyone from Phlegm actually realized that they were involved in a war) and all the chaos from the rats had died down, he was off. Somewhere. Anywhere. Soon. Ten years was quite enough. Dullitch was far too strange a kingdom, especially at night. Weird screams would erupt from nowhere, hideous twisted cries of people facing horror without mercy. Modeset was beginning to recognize some of them by pitch. The low, continuous moans were usually caused by the Burrow Street Trolls leaping on some poor unsuspecting beggar, while the higher wailings were caused by young ladies running into Jock the Toddler, a fiend who stalked the streets of Dullitch after sundown, preying on women. He hadn't actually murdered anyone, but a greengrocer's wife had some nasty nips on her ankles.

A door slammed somewhere off to the east. Modeset crossed to the arch windows and peered out into the murky midnight gloom, but he couldn't see very far in front of his hands for the fog. A second door slammed, followed by a third and a fourth. Modeset rolled his eyes: perhaps it was a contest of some sort. This city had some curious idiosyncrasies; it wouldn't surprise him. He produced a woolly hat from his robe pocket, took up his candlestick, and wandered down to the dungeons.

Only two of the cells below Dullitch Palace were occupied. The first contained Elee Klias, a geriatric woman who muttered constantly on the subject of vintage wines and the encouragement of nudity. Presumably, old Duke Culver had imprisoned her for the latter. Modeset ignored her incessant whining and went straight to the second cell.

As he flung open the door, his frame illuminated a pillory inside of which struggled a trembling figure. Modeset used his candle to light three further brackets before turning to face the small, wizened face of Rochus the Soak.

"Evening, seer," Modeset said calmly. "How are they treating you down here?"

Rochus coughed and spluttered. "Thou shalt pay for this. . . ."

"Really? An unfortunate attitude, for you were to be released tomorrow."

"Ha! Empty words!" grumbled Rochus. "I've never encountered such insolence in my life."

"Mmm?" said Modeset, a smug grin on his face.

"Thou'lt swing from the yardarm for this."

"Oh, do be quiet, man! Surely you're not still under the delusion that you're some kind of god?"

"I am a great deity, like my father before me," said Rochus proudly.

Modeset tried to invoke images of Anglucian the Soak. From what he could remember, the man had been a notorious womanizer, but had little to boast about in the divinity department. A reputation for scampering across battlements pursued by furious husbands didn't exactly paint a portrait of heavenly nobility. Furthermore, Modeset found it difficult to recall ever seeing the Great Soak with his britches on.

"Well, now that you mention your father—"

"Silence!" cried Rochus. "Thy lips seal thy doom."

"How amusing," said Modeset. "Tell me, are you going to give me the information I require voluntarily, or am I going to have to take another set of pins to your fingernails?"

This question caused Rochus to lapse into a choking fit.

"So, great seer," the duke continued, raising his eyebrows. "What is going on in my decrepit city? A single word will suffice, as long as it's accurate. Conspiracy, perhaps? Some devilish form of rodent warfare from Legrash?"

Rochus's cracked lips trembled, parted. "M-m-magic," he whispered. "Dark, terrible magic."

Modeset nodded, rose. As he closed the dungeon door, the soak began to cry.

"Show us your winter warmers!" screamed Elee, from the next cell.

Diek marched through the streets of Dullitch, an insane smile on his face and a bizarre melody rising from his flute. Behind him, a group of young children stumbled along, chuckling with a strange merriment, their eyes glazed over. They had staggered out from houses on all sides of the city, appearing at doors and windows, staggering over narrow lanes and stumbling along through dark alleys to find the source of the tune. This oblivious little band was joined by others, and the group became a troop, then a regiment and, finally, an army, all trotting obediently after the stranger with the marvelous music. Soon, they were gone, leaving only the odd cap and a handful of shoes behind them.

The bells of Dullitch struck midnight. . . .

A short distance from Dullitch, Gordo Goldeaxe sat beside a small campfire and gnawed his way through a chicken leg. Groan and Tambor were sleeping and, despite the fact that their combined snore could have penetrated the eardrums of a man some sixty miles away, Gordo wasn't paying them any undue attention. This was because, for the last half an hour, he had been watching a vast cloud form over the city. It was a magical cloud, he felt sure, because it crackled with energy and glowed alternately white and purple against a backdrop of darkness.

It was also very, very unsettling. Gordo had heard about such atmospheric oddities, of course, and how they formed in an area where gargantuan amounts of magic were being used. But something about this particular buildup was making him wish he'd taken first watch of the evening.

The screams started just after sunrise, and again Modeset put them down to good old-fashioned Dullitch eccentricity. It was only when he came downstairs for breakfast that he realized things were a little more serious. As he descended the small flight of steps leading to the Great Hall, an entourage of city officials alighted on him like vultures on a corpse. Pegrand was nowhere to be seen.

"They broke down my door!" yelled Quaris Sands, the Home Secretary, above the fray.

"They've demanded we hang you, Duke Modeset!" added another voice.

Pegrand appeared at the doorway, pushed his way inside and slammed the portal. "There's a rabble outside, milord," he shouted. "It looks like half the city."

Everyone began speaking at once.

Duke Modeset raised his hand for silence; to his surprise it worked. "One at a time," he began, offering the group a reassuring smile. "Pegrand, you first. Why is there a rabble outside?"

"It's that countrysider, milord," said his manservant. "Two beggars saw him on Stainer Street and—"

"Doing what?"

"Taking the children."

Modeset frowned. "What children?"

"All of them, milord. In the night, like a thief."

"But, how?"

"Same way he got the rats, by all accounts. Played a tune and they followed him."

"And the militiaman on duty at the time?"

Pegrand swallowed, hard. "Chap named Phelt, milord," he said breathily. "He fell asleep. I think he'd been drinking."

"I see," said Modeset, turning his attention to the rest of the group. "You, with your hand up, you wish to say something?"

Quaris Sands nodded. "I'm afraid that the Yowler churches, as well as several other religious establishments, have issued statements condemning the situation. If matters are not put in order by Friday, there will be repercussions."

"I see," said Modeset, solemnly. "Does anybody else have something to contribute?"

"I do," said Chancellor Quarry. "Understandably, people are beside themselves with distress and confusion; however, there is a third party inciting them to riot."

"A third party?"

"Yes, milord. A young lad came back on his own, said he'd been under the musical spell, but he hadn't been fast enough to keep up with the rest. He's lame in one leg, you see."

"Hmm . . . interesting. Did he happen to see where the foreigner was headed?"

"Not really, milord. I mean, only the direction—"

"Right, and can we make any guesses based on that?" asked the duke.

"A few. There's not many places he could take them without passing through one of the villages, and we'd have heard of that already. Of course, there's a lot of forest out there, and mountains, I'll grant you."

"Your guess then, Mr. Quarry?"

"Well, if it was *me*—not that I'd kidnap a load of kids—"

"Of course not," said Modeset. "Please continue."

"But if I *did*, and I wanted to get a ransom or something, I'd go for one of the big mountains. Lot of blind spots, see, caves and such. You could hide an army up there. Mind you, Great Rise is a good day and a half away, so I'd hedge bets against *that*. The Twelve is nearer, and it's the biggest mountain this side of Phlegm."

"Right, well, at least we've got a few possibles to go on. Now, about the lame boy. Doesn't it seem strange to you that this lone youth broke the spell *and* returned unscathed?"

Quarry took a deep breath. "Apart from the leg, you mean?"

"You said he was lame anyway!"

"Yes, Duke Modeset, but I just don't think . . ."

There was a disapproving murmur from the gathered officials, but Modeset forged on, regardless. "So there's the chance of a conspiracy between the boy and the foreigner?"

"Um . . . no . . . not unless you think he's intentionally inciting a riot, milord."

A smile spread slowly across the duke's face. "Exactly! You see? Now you know what to suggest. I'll keep an eye on this boy during your speech."

"M-m-my speech?" stuttered Quarry.

Modeset clapped his hands together and motioned to two of the palace guards. They marched into the fray of city officials and each snatched one of the chancellor's arms.

"Pegrand," the duke went on. "Have a scroll nailed to every notice board in the city. There's to be a public announcement and, soon," he continued, smiling, "a public execution. Mr. Sands, assemble the council and prepare a statement to satisfy all the parents in Dullitch that their children will be returned."

Modeset peered over a collection of muttering heads. "I'll have my breakfast now, Pegrand," he added.

The diamond clock on Crest Hill chimed eleven.

Quaris Sands, who'd had to stand in for Tambor Forestall when the chairman had failed to arrive, shuffled a ream of parchment and leaned forward across the table. From what little he could make out, only a few members of the council had bothered to turn up. "Right," began Quaris.

"Go on—"

"Well—"

"Yes?"

"The fact is—"

"What?"

He narrowed his eyes at the troglodyte translator, whom he'd patiently observed at the last meeting. Its long warty nose still dripped a horrid mucus that burned holes in the new oak table and smelled acrid. Quaris stared around the room and noticed that the orc representative was absent. "Where's that fella you're translating for?" he asked. "There's no point in your being here if he's not present. You might as well disappear."

The troglodyte smiled. "I'm part of the council now, official-like. I joined yesterday."

"You can't be a member," said Quaris, shaking his head at the little creature.

"The duke's secretary seemed to think I could," said the translator, holding something under Quaris's nose. "He gave me this scroll. It's signed and everything."

"So it is," said Quaris, with a defeated sigh.

"So I'm a member now, right?"

A crowd of spectators was widening around him.

Play the other tune, Diek, The Voice went on. *They deserve it. There is a place, a secret place of which I am aware. Take your revenge and I can lead you there. No one will ever find them, Diek. No one will ever find them. . . .*

"It would appear that is the case."

"My mum'll be proud. She always wanted me to go into politics. I remember when I was little she used to say—"

The chairman closed his eyes and prayed for patience. "Right," he snapped. "I'd like to call to order the, er, latest meeting of the Dullitch Council. We're gathered here today—"

"Sounds like the start of a funeral," interrupted the translator.

"—to compose a speech for Duke Modeset," Quaris continued. "To address to the citizens of our fair city."

The translator shuddered. "That's going to be tricky," it said.

"I wonder if I may make a suggestion," said Taciturn Cadrick.

Everyone stared at him expectantly. "Perhaps," he continued, "we could blame transdimensional demonics."

A collection of blank faces gave not the merest indication of understanding.

"That is to say, the infringement of demons into our civilized society. Something very similar happened a while back, when I was Trade Minister for Legrash."

"What's that got to do with kidnapped children?" asked Quaris, with a frown.

"Quite a lot, actually," said Cadrick, taking a deep breath. "I believe that Diek Wustapha has been possessed by a despicable demonic fiend."

This didn't engender quite the reaction he was expecting.

"A show of hands for Mr. Cadrick's suggestion?" Quris ventured.

Only two went up, and they both belonged to Taciturn.

"Right," said Quaris. "Then that's firmly voted down. Anyone else?"

"How about this," said the translator, rummaging in his satchel and producing a roll of parchment which he then proceeded to unravel. "Citizens of Dullitch. There has been a terrible catastrophe, but I, your duke, and the honorable members of your City Council have come up with a solution. We have dispatched a hunting party to find the stolen children and bring the terrible fiend who has abducted them to justice."

Quaris opened his mouth and closed it again. A few members at the other end of the table clapped their hands in approval. Taciturn Cadrick rested his chin on his hands and tried to look miserable.

"Excellent," Quaris managed. "Where did you say you were from?"

"I didn't," said the translator, his candlewax nose disgorging another globule of mucus. "And, besides, it's not perfect. For a start, we don't *have* a hunting party."

An air of gloom settled over the table.

Taciturn Cadrick was the first to speak. "How about that barbarian fellow in the Rotting Ferret the other night? The one with the dwarf?"

"No," said Quaris firmly. "They came at the city's request and we told them to get lost. They're hardly likely to help us now. Besides, they've probably left already. They're bound to be miles away."

Taciturn shook his head.

"Pity. They had our chairman with 'em too."

"Tambor?"

"Yes: Chas Firebrand told me."

Quaris was still shaking his head. "Tambor Forestall socializing with mercenaries?" he gasped, as if the very thought were abhorrent to him.

"Absolutely, and he got a fair bit of ale down him, I'd say. In fact, I think I heard Chas Firebrand say something about his leaving the city with them."

"Well, that's fantastic," Quaris snapped, glaring at the Trade Minister with naked distaste. "How unutterably superb! Our chairman has run off to join a mercenary band. That's just rosy, isn't it?

Does anybody actually feel like pretending to be a member of the council, you know, just for the afternoon?"

He turned to the troglodyte translator. "What did you say your name was?"

It shrugged. "I guess you can call me Burnie."

"Burnie," repeated Quaris. "Send a message to the Rooftop Runners. I wish to speak with a young man called Jimmy Quickstint."

Three hours later, Duke Modeset sat in the throne room of Dullitch Palace and gazed down at an exhausted Quaris Sands.

"You really must do something about those stairs, milord," the acting chairman managed between puffs. "I can't see me lasting long in my new post if I keep having to mission it up here every afternoon."

"I didn't *build* the palace, Mr. Sands," Modeset pointed out. "And I certainly don't have enough money to call in the stonework specialists."

"Ah yes . . . um . . . humble apologies, but I think they're called masons."

"Whatever," snapped Modeset. "You have my speech?"

"Indeed. And a progress report, my lord."

The duke raised one eyebrow.

Quaris fought on. "It appears that we have in fact formulated a plan."

"Really? How splendid," said Modeset.

"Yes. We, that is, the council, have decided to send a hunting party after the villain."

"A hunting party?" The duke smiled. "How traditional."

Quaris nodded. "A powerful sorcerer who, until recently, was in fact, um, a city dignitary and, um, hopefully, the two mercenaries you met yourself. There's only one problem," he added.

"Which is?" said the duke, impatiently.

"They've already left the city. We've found the, um, *sorcerer's* grandson: he's a trainee member of the Rooftop Runners. He thinks they may still be on the Dullitch road, and he's agreed to go after them and ask for help."

Modeset scratched his chin thoughtfully before continuing. "So, in point of fact, we have hired a hunting party that doesn't yet realize it is either hired or that it *is* a hunting party. Splendid work. By the way you're staring at your feet, I assume there is a problem even with this pitiable lack of a plan?"

"Well, as you say, milord," Quaris went on. "The problem is that they're bound to ask why the Wustupha lad kidnapped the children. And when Jimmy, that's the grandson, tells them it was because you didn't pay him, they're hardly likely to trip themselves up in a rescue attempt, are they, milord?"

The duke relaxed, flexed his arms, and offered Quaris a wry smile. "Not a problem, Mr. Sands. When does this 'Jimmy' leave?"

"In approximately . . ." Quaris stared out of the eastern arch toward the diamond clock on Crest Hill, "one hour."

"I see. Then give him this to take with him."

Duke Modeset rose purposefully, marched through a door in the north wall, and reappeared carrying two small but heavy-looking pouches. He tossed them to Quaris and went back for another two.

"There are more than a hundred crowns in each pouch," he said. "They'll get a further five hundred each, if and when they return the children unharmed, and have disposed of this young freak."

"May I ask where all this money came from, milord?" asked Quaris, eyeing the heavy pouches.

"Certainly," said Modeset. "The good chancellor was looking after some of it for the greater prosperity of the city. In a room above the silversmith's on Furly Lane, I might add."

"I'll make sure the boy gets going as soon as possible," said Quaris.

"Can we trust a thief with the city's entire gold reserve, do you think?"

"I don't think we've got much choice, Duke Modeset."

"Quite right. Let's just hope Quarry's execution will satisfy the crowd. Oh, and Mr. Sands?"

Quaris hesitated at the door, turned and raised an eyebrow. "Milord?"

"This dignitary turned sorcerer . . . it wouldn't be Tambor Forestall, by any chance?"

"Oh no, er, um, no, my word, absolutely not . . ."

"That's a yes, then, is it?" asked the duke.

"I'm afraid so, my lord," answered Quaris.

"I feared as much. You are excused."

Quaris muttered something unintelligible under his breath, and ambled off.

FOURTEEN

CHARCOAL CLOUDS gathered over the Varick Pass, hung there motionless for a time, and then began to spit all over the place like the worst kind of ball player.

Low-lying cloud formations encircled the tallest peaks. It was said that, upon reaching the summit of the Twelve, a man could be forgiven for thinking that he had entered a land of balding giants. Patches of sparse woodland dotted the mountainsides, where a few of the region's more unsociable dwarf tribes lived.

These wooded areas were also frequented by trolls, ogres, and the occasional wandering Notjusyeti (a strange beast with big feet and a tendency to keep mountaineers waiting).

High on a rocky path, approximately halfway up the Twelve, Diek Wustapha stopped dead before a rock wall and listened. Moments before, he'd emerged from the clouds like an apparition, stepping through thin air as if descending an invisible staircase. The children had followed in a straight, orderly line, their eyes focused on some distant preoccupation.

And, still, Diek listened.

A number of the smaller children careened into him, their zombielike eyes wide. Diek pushed them back, drew in a breath, and raised his arms. The voice that came forth was not his own.

"Eliumariss toomathane. Rastarinimpetus kadant!"

For a time, nothing happened. Diek just stood motionless before the rock face, his hands shaking from the sheer mental effort the spell required. He took a few tentative steps, then strode right through the barrier as though it had never existed. One by one, the children followed him beyond the wall and down, down into the darkness.

Far below, Gordo had decided to go around the base

of the Twelve, but this had turned out to be a very unfortunate choice in terms of their progress. Their problems had begun with a chance meeting with a group of nomads who had set up camp in the gargantuan mountain's lower foothills. The nomads mixed warm hospitality with a seemingly endless supply of ale. Consequently, the group had been in their company for the best part of a day. Now, thanks to some friendly nomad advice about the dangerous creatures lurking on the Twelve's eastern base, they'd elected to go *over* the mountain instead. To do this successfully, Tambor had reasoned, they needed to start from the well-worn path that they had been on the day before, and that meant starting the whole journey over again from scratch. During these difficult hours, they spent much of their journey retracing their steps in hushed silence (or at least the sort of silence that's regularly interrupted by muffled curses).

A glimmer on the horizon signaled that thunder was lurking and a bitter wind whistled down the path, making progress as difficult as possible.

"I don't suppose either of you carries a readable map of the area?" Tambor said, his teeth chattering in the wind.

Groan and Gordo stared blankly at each other. Then they cast a glance in every direction, hoping to

see some signs of a path that wouldn't involve con-
quering the mountain.

"I take it that's a no, then?" the old man continued.

"Oh, look at this," Gordo replied. "It's not
enough that we've landed up with a sorcerer with no
spell book, now he's whining along the way!"

Tambor averted his eyes. He had a rolled-up carpet under one arm, which he'd collected from his
lodgings in Laker Street. It was a magic carpet, he'd
assured them, but one that definitely wouldn't support
a man of Groan's size and stature. He had just been
preparing to roll the carpet out, when he'd
remembered his missing spell book and the not insub-
stantial conjuration that was required to start the
thing.

Gordo spat at the grass and fiddled with a strap
beneath his helmet. Eventually it became unhooked.

"We should go back," said Gordo. "I saw something
last night that I didn't much like the look of. I think
there was a magic—"

"Damn magic," said Groan. "An' damn the city.
'S never done us no favors."

"I just thought maybe we could have a look—"

"You're goin' soft, Gordo Goldeaxe," said Groan.

"I am not!" the dwarf protested, taking instant
offence at the use of his full name. "But we don't know

where we're going! You might walk the land, Groan Teethgrit, but some of us have homes and families that love and care for a dwarf . . . who brings home gold for the village."

He dropped his battle-axe, slumped onto a rotting tree stump, and began beating himself over the head with the dangling chinstrap of his helmet. "I'm fed up with this traveling lark," he said. "I wish I'd stayed in the village with the rest of my tribe. Uncle Grimson always said I was crazy to be a mercenary."

"There might be a friendly village in the foothills," said Tambor. Groan sniffed and peered up at the Twelve.

A flash of lightning lit up the sky.

"There'd better be," said Gordo, snatching up his battle-axe.

A knowledge of geography is always useful when traveling on foot, but the odd trio carefully negotiating the Twelve weren't too hot on geography (Groan suspected it had something to do with keeping fit). And, unlike Diek, they didn't have the advantage of being aided by dark magic.

They were a quarter of the way up the mountain, when Groan suddenly stopped them dead in their tracks.

"Don't like it 'ere," said Groan. "It's too quiet. I reckon they're all waitin' in the trees to jump out at us."

"Who?" asked Tambor, looking blindly around.

"Them." Groan sniffed. As far as he was concerned "us" was whoever he was with and "them" was anybody else. Gordo swung his battle-axe experimentally.

An arrow landed in the grass beside the path. Upright.

"'S an arrow," announced Groan, in case anyone had missed it.

No one moved. A few seconds passed without incident. Somewhere off among the trees, a shadow shifted. Tambor took this as his cue to make a definite exit and dove into a convenient bush at the side of the path. Three more arrows rained down upon the group.

"I'd just like to point out," whispered Tambor from his bush, "that I think you can take the bravery thing a bit too far."

"I've got little to worry about," said Gordo, out of the corner of his mouth. "Small target."

Tambor muttered something under his breath and tried to dig a hole beneath the bush by scooping out mounds of dirt with his hands.

"Coward," said Groan.

Gordo grimaced. Four arrows was fair indication of trouble. "What is it, d'you think?" asked Gordo, staring at the barbarian hopefully. "Trolls? Orcs?"

A fifth arrow landed just beyond Tambor's bush, making the sorcerer yelp.

Groan shook his head. "Too 'igh for orcs," he said. "Too low fer trolls."

"Great," whispered Tambor. "Now we know who's definitely *not* attacking us. Any chance of a guess in the opposite direction? I'd just like to know who to curse when I'm picking an arrowhead out of my aaaarrhh . . . !"

The sorcerer leaped out of his bush, danced around in circles for a few seconds, and then dove back in.

"What was that?" asked Gordo.

Tambor coughed. "Hedgehog," he snapped. "Can't you two find somewhere to hide?"

"It's okay," said Gordo. "I think they might've gone."

"Don't be ridiculous!" said Tambor. "You don't fire five arrows at someone and then just walk away."

Groan shrugged. "P'raps it's a greetin'," he said.

"Very friendly," said Tambor. "I don't fancy visiting *their* village." He shivered at the thought.

"You know somethin'," Gordo said, grinning.

"You're actually startin' to think like us. Isn't he, Groan?"

"Yeah," the barbarian agreed. "We're c'ruptin' 'im."

Suddenly, the rain intensified, turning from thin drizzle into a heavy shower.

Tambor sneezed and flicked away some of the rain-water dripping from the brim of his hat. He was just about to start complaining, when the sixth arrow arrived.

Jimmy Quickstint galloped on down the road. It was nice of the duke to lend him this wonderful horse, he thought.

Mountains loomed ahead. Jimmy tried to think clearly. Presuming the two mercenaries were still with his granddad, they would probably have headed for Legrash. He looked up at the mountains and decided that no fool would attempt to climb something they could go around. After a lengthy struggle, he managed to point the horse toward a patch of forest around the base of the Twelve. Then he reached down and slapped it on the flank, which turned out to be a big mistake, as he fell off.

"Come back!" Jimmy shouted, waving his arms frantically as the horse galloped back toward Dullitch. "Please! I need. . . . Oh no, somebody help!"

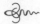

He stood and watched as the knight's steed became a speck on the horizon. Then he looked round at the forest, sat down cross-legged, and began to sob.

"You said orcs wouldn't be this far up!" Tambor screamed. He was sprinting up and down the path with remarkable speed for a man of more than eighty years. A short distance away Groan was slamming heads together, six at a time in some cases.

"Maybe these orcs are different!" shouted Gordo, swinging his battle-axe around a widening circle of greenskins. "You know, the ambitious type or something—"

"Ambitious orcs?" yelled Tambor. "Well that's just terrific, isn't it?" He ducked down as a saber whistled past.

A screech echoed from above and a garji-rider swooped low over the mountainside. Garjis were terrible creatures, half snake and half dragon, that were regularly harnessed and ridden by their orcish masters.

Groan took one look up at the treetops and dashed off into the woods at the side of the road.

"Where are you going?" screamed Tambor.

"Get a tree to fro' at 'em!" the barbarian shouted back.

Gordo was doing what he always did in battle;

silently promising the dwarf gods that, should he escape now, he would never leave his village again. Divine intervention came in the form of a large pebble, which he tripped on, narrowly avoiding a saber hurled by one of the greenskins. Lucky, Gordo thought, but I'd have preferred a lightning bolt or something.

Groan came thundering out of the woods, a small tree balanced on one shoulder. He stopped running, reached back, and pitched it at the winged monstrosity. It missed. Again, Groan turned to run.

"Where are you going now?" screamed Tambor, who was perched on the lowest branch of a nearby oak.

"Get annuva one!" shouted Groan.

"We haven't got time!" yelled Gordo, above the fray. "Besides, you'd probably miss again."

Groan scowled. "Never missed anyfin' twice," he said. Never hit anyfin' twice, he thought.

Tambor had experienced a sudden flash of inspiration. Maybe he could get the carpet working if he remembered exactly the right words. He felt around beside him but his fingers just found bark. He thought, The carpet's still in the bush. He peered over at Gordo, who was struggling against a greenskin waving what looked like a shovel.

"Hey, Gordo! Could you pass me my carpet?"

The dwarf's reply was lost on the wind, which was probably for the best.

Gordo's battle-axe flew through the air and buried itself in the stomach of the garji, whose rider screamed and dove off. Tambor shrieked, Gordo smiled and ran to retrieve his weapon, and even Groan looked momentarily taken aback. The elation didn't last for long. A cold scream echoed round the mountain as a second group of greenskins poured into the clearing, scrambling over one another in an attempt to draw first blood.

Gordo's battle-axe danced in a complicated arc around him, opening gashes and lopping off limbs, while Groan was employing half a branch to swat away the brave few who dared approach him. However, their numbers were increasing, and Tambor fancied that he could make out a second line of orcs in the shadows around the clearing. Even with Groan as a deterrent, he had to admit the situation didn't look good.

FIFTEEN

WHAT JIMMY had taken to be a forest was unexpectedly turning out to be more of a jungle.

Incredible, he thought. Outside it's freezing cold and in here it's like the oven of the gods. It would be fair to say that he was not enjoying the beauty of the wild. He didn't know which was worse, losing the royal horse or losing all the money intended to lure the mercenaries back. Time was probably running out for the children of Dullitch and here he was, stranded in some dense wilderness, without any hope of ever finding the mercenaries, and no money to pay them even if he did! The whole day had been one big disaster. Come to think about it, his whole *life* was one big disaster.

He coughed and swatted away a few mosquitoes.

There were trees in every direction. He imagined a pair of eyes beneath every twig, hissing and biting at anything that didn't qualify as a member of the same species which, in a jungle of this size, amounted to just about everything. A crescendo of unpleasant sounds was building in the distance, as a pack of unknown terrors hunted down some poor primate. He expected an explosion of jagged claws and needle-sharp teeth at any moment. Instead, a small, featherless monstrosity of nameless origin squawked a hideous cacophony from a nearby tree. I'm lost, he thought. That's the second time I've been past that tree with the red arrow scrawled on it.

He tripped over a tree root, then gave it a vengeful kick. A branch that lay horizontally across the path opened half an eye and slithered away behind a tree stump. Jimmy shivered; he'd had a dreadful fear of snakes ever since his grandfather had told him that his favorite uncle had been strangled by a feather boa.

The recollection didn't do much to calm his nerves. The quicker he got out of this place, he thought, the better.

Jimmy was, in fact, struggling through the Carafat

Jungle, north of Dullitch, which played host to some of the oldest (and indeed most terrible) tribes in Illmoor. The Carif Backslashers, Gib's Minions, the winged hordes of Yud the Acolyte, Trumnf Caew's Marauders— they all had a stake here. Wander into this territory by accident, and you were lucky to last five minutes.

These jungles housed spear traps triggered by a spit in the wrong direction, death mazes where twisted minds painted misleading arrows on the walls using their own blood, and freak log slides that could roll you flatter than a pancake. In Carafat, the only thing more dangerous than standing still was moving.

Jimmy had heard mention of a handful of notorious expeditions, the most successful of which had been one led by a man called Passion. After months of torture at the hands of a mysterious heathen death squad, Passion had returned with some insightful advice to all would-be travelers. Unfortunately, it was stapled to his head and written in hieroglyphs, so no one ever found out what it meant.

Something large with no shortage of feathers flew in Jimmy's face, and he reached up and smacked it aside. It hit a sweating palm tree and spent the next few seconds hobbling around on the floor. Jimmy stepped away from the creature and took a good look. It wasn't surprising

Dullitch didn't have an aviary. There really wasn't much to like about birds, he decided. Especially birds of prey. Where was the connection, for goodness' sake? He tried to think of a sacred psalm with the word *vulture* in it, but came up empty-handed.

A vine swung loose from a nearby tree and dangled provocatively in front of him. I'm not falling for *that* one, he thought.

The path he was following ended rather abruptly at a rock face. It looked false. Jimmy cocked his head and closed one eye, a habit of his that kicked in whenever he had to size up a situation. There was definitely the outline of a door there, a sort of rectangle etched into the stone. He pushed gently, then put all his weight against it to give him proper leverage. There was a tiny creak, screech, and an unrelated rumble in the distance; apart from that, nothing happened. He swore under his breath, stepped back and gave the slab an experimental kick. To his surprise, this worked wonders. . . .

Several tons of rock slid away, revealing a small portal and a set of dusty stairs leading down into darkness.

Far, far below, deep inside the heart of the Twelve, Diek Wustapha stood atop a rock in a draughty chasm. Below him, a sea of tiny faces stared upward, eyes glazed, captivated by the magic that swirled around him. It was visible now, a frenzied purple cloud sprinkled liberally with glittering, frozen stars.

Acceding to the wishes of The Voice, Diek Wustapha raised the flute to his lips and began to play.

A hum went up from his young audience, resonating around the chasm like the echo of a wind chime dropped down a deep and resonant well.

All the life we need is here, Diek, said The Voice in its terrible tones. *On the power of these young minds, we can exist for centuries. We can . . . rise again, as powerful as once we were. You have done well, Diek. You have done well. . . .*

SIXTEEN

IT HAD TAKEN FIFTEEN orc warriors to drag Groan to the ground and another three to clap him in irons. Gordo had put up a fair fight himself, eventually overcome by four heavy greenskin scouts. Tambor came a little more easily; in fact, he'd surrendered even before the orcs had noticed him.

The tribal chieftain arrived to look over his prisoners. He was a grotty little orc, stout of gut and long of tooth, with enough souvenirs dangling from around his neck to intimate that he ran a very successful outfit.

He prodded Groan in the arm, spat at Tambor,

and gave Gordo a sharp kick in the ribs. Then he snatched up the dwarf's battle-axe and waved his arm in the direction of the wood. A succession of mumbles died away and the tribe began to move.

"Psst," said Tambor. His arms were chained to a sort of log pulley-system without the log. "Psst!"

Groan continued to walk with his head down. The rest of his body was constricted by chains.

"Hey!"

The barbarian glanced over at Tambor. "Yeah?" he said.

"Do you think you could break your chains?"

"Dunno," answered Groan.

"Why don't you try, then?"

"Try what?"

Tambor rolled his eyes. He had a feeling he could spend the rest of his life having this conversation. "Why don't you try to break your chains?" he whispered.

"With what?"

"Forget I mentioned it," said Tambor, shaking his head.

The chains were beginning to grind on Tambor's hands. He yelped and then hurried to catch up with his captor.

Gordo was having a slightly easier time of it.

Apparently none of the orcs had been prepared to walk along bending over, so they'd made some kind of platform for him to stand on.

Tambor struggled against his chains and got a sharp slap in the face for his efforts. He waited until his head had stopped spinning, then turned and gave Gordo a half-smile.

"I expect you've been orc-napped a few times, eh?" he said. "Incidentally, do you know the one about the mongoose and—"

"Shut it, coward," grumbled Groan.

"Well, that's nice, isn't it?" said Tambor. "Considering I'm about to save us all from certain death."

Gordo turned a beady eye on the sorcerer. Even Groan listened in.

"I think," said Tambor, twitching to relieve an itch in his beard, "that I may be able to remember a very good offensive spell."

Groan sniffed. He hated magic.

"What's that?" said Gordo suspiciously.

"It's called Tower of Screaming Doom," said Tambor. "If I can do it right, a spinning column twenty feet tall should appear in the air and wipe out anyone standing."

"Well, can you do it or not?" asked Gordo, excitedly.

"I think so."

Groan heard the sorcerer mumble something in a foreign tongue.

"When I say *now*," Tambor whispered. "I want you both to dive for the ground."

The mercenaries murmured in agreement.

"Now!"

Tambor muttered an incantation and dove theatrically to the ground as a spinning column of flame winked into existence above him. It soared high over the heads of the tallest orcs, but no one paid very much attention. The spinning column was approximately five inches high.

Groan used the momentary confusion to break his chains. Orcs flew in all directions.

Gordo leaped from his platform down onto Tambor's captor. The Tower of Screaming Doom devastated a nearby beehive before fizzling out.

Jimmy Quickstint peered into the shadowy darkness lurking just beyond the first few steps. The way he saw it, there were two choices. He could either turn back, run home to Dullitch and face the wrath of Duke Modeset, or he could go ahead on the chance that the portal would stay open, in case he decided to run back after all. Simple, really.

He reached out a tentative foot and brought it

down on the top step. Nothing happened. Then he stepped inside. A flock of birds erupted from the tree-tops behind, and he spun around, breathing heavily. Nothing happened.

Jimmy swallowed and offered a silent prayer to the god of ignorant thieves, hoping that there was one. Then he closed his eyes, clenched his fists and descended the first three steps. Nothing happened. Thank the lords for that, he thought, leaning against the inner wall. Perhaps there really was a god looking out for him, after all.

Something in the Stygian gloom below made a *crraaawwl* noise. Jimmy froze with fear, just as the stone slab behind him rolled back into place and locked with a decisive click.

"That was a close one," said Tambor, staring around the clearing with a satisfied smile. "Good thing I know my business."

The battle in the woods was over. It had drawn to a swift conclusion when Groan had happened upon the tactic of using one orc to hit another. He brushed a moldy leaf off his shoulder and flexed. "Good fight," he said, grinning.

"Yep," said Tambor. "Don't mess with magic, that's what I say."

"Magic?" exclaimed Gordo, leaning on his battle-axe. "You didn't *do* anything!"

Tambor looked amazed. "What about the Tower of Screaming Doom!" he shouted.

"What about it?" snapped Gordo.

"Didn't you see it? It flew around for ages!"

"I saw it," said Groan. "Smacked it over that way."

He pointed over at a twisted oak tree, where half a beehive was smoldering.

"Idiots!" said Tambor, shaking his fists. "That was earth magic at work, that was! Will somebody get me out of these chains!"

"*Croaaarrrkk!*"

Jimmy started at the sound, took half a step back, then slipped and tumbled head over heels down the staircase. He landed at the bottom in an awkward heap.

When a few seconds had passed without anything biting a chunk from his ankle, he forced himself up on to his elbows and began to look around.

Spent torches hung from ancient braziers on the walls. From what he could make out, he was on a landing of some kind. There was a cell in the far wall. It had one occupant.

"What a spot of luck," the man said, stretching out

a hand between the bars of his prison. "Thought we were goners, we did."

Jimmy boggled at him. "Who are you?" he asked.

"I'm Stump, and this here is Mick. We're prisoners, as you've probably guessed."

Jimmy strained to look inside the cage. He couldn't see anything. "Is there somebody else in there with you?" he asked.

Stump peered around behind him. "Nah," he said. "It's just me and Mick." A flake of dust fell out of his beard. "Doubt if there'd be room in here for three of us," he added.

"How long have you been in there?" asked Jimmy.

"A while, I reckon. Mick was here already."

"Who locked you up?"

"Oh, nobody *locked* us up," said Stump. "These caves are old, really old, and the tribes that used to lurk hereabouts had a habit of diggin' out long tunnels and plungin' pits all over the surface above. I fell through like a good'un. Serves me right for not lookin' where I was goin. Reckon you could get us out?"

Jimmy nodded. "No problem, there isn't a lock in the land I can't break."

Gordo wiped some green slime from the head of his battle-axe. The temperature was dropping rapidly and a thin mist had begun to coil among the trees. The forest was becoming darker and gloomier by the minute.

"See all the crushed twigs?" said Gordo. "I reckon this place is crawling with orcs, and we certainly don't want any more surprises."

Groan suddenly snatched hold of Tambor and flung him into the lower branches of the nearest tree.

"What was *that* for?" snapped the sorcerer, dangling precariously from the branches. "Have you any idea how old I am?"

"Climb up, tell us what you see," commanded Gordo.

"What, all the way to the top?"

"Yeah," said Groan.

"We should be careful," Gordo whispered, when Tambor was three-quarters of the way to the top. "He is getting on, you know."

"I've bin' thinkin' 'bout that," said Groan. "Did you see the way he jumped for that bush out on the road?"

"So?" Gordo said, brows furrowed. He didn't like it when the barbarian started to think for himself.

"I reckon there's somefin' goin' on there," said Groan suspiciously. "I don't reckon he's as old as he makes out."

"But he's got to be!" said Gordo. "I mean, I

remember he was quite famous when I first came to Dullitch, way back. Tambor Forestall! Everyone knew about Tambor Forestall back then. I'm sure of it. Tambor Forestall and the Seven Dragons, Tambor Forestall and the Trolls of Epsworth Creek, Tambor Forestall and, and . . ."

"And the Tower of Screamin' Doom?" ventured Groan. He smiled; sarcasm was a new experience for him.

Tambor was slowly descending from the top of the tree. He slipped on one of the lower branches and landed on the forest floor with a crash.

"Well," he said eventually, "there's good news and there's bad news. Which do you want first?"

Gordo shrugged. "Either."

"Right," Tambor continued, getting to his feet. "The good news is, we've lost the orcs. The bad news is, we have to go back the way we came."

"Why would we want to do that?" exclaimed Gordo.

"Because there happens to be a giant chopping wood about two clearings ahead of us."

"A giant?" said Gordo.

"Yes. G–i–a–n–t. Giant. He's twice the size of Groan." The old sorcerer shook his head. "I suppose he might be friendly, but I doubt it. Either way, we can't take the risk."

"We won't then," Groan muttered. "I'll just knock 'im out."

"What?" Tambor gasped, looking down at Gordo. "Did you hear that? He's out of his stupid mind. That's a giant, for crying out loud. He'll get us all killed."

The dwarf shrugged. "Stay here if you like," he said, unclasping his battle-axe. "I doubt this'll take long."

"Hey!" Tambor called after them. "Is there any chance of dashing back to fetch my carpet?"

Deep inside the Twelve there was a barely audible *clink* and the prison door swung open.

"That's incredible!" said Stump. "We're impressed."

Jimmy was about to point out that he couldn't actually see anybody else in the cell, when another question came to mind. "You haven't seen anything unusual since you've been in here, have you?" Jimmy asked.

Stump squinted back at the cage. "Like what?" said Stump.

"Well, like an eight-foot-tall barbarian, an old sorcerer, and a dwarf," answered Jimmy, hopefully.

"Nope, sorry," said Stump, smiling. "Haven't seen

anyone like that. Don't know about Mick; he was
already down here when I arrived. He might've seen
somethin'. You can ask him yourself."

Jimmy smiled at Stump sympathetically. "Insanity's
a terrible thing," he muttered.

"What's that?"

"Er . . . I said it must've been horrible to be locked
up down here all that time."

"Oh, not really," said Stump, shaking his head.
"We kept ourselves busy, you know how it is." He
scratched a stubbly upper lip. "The first few days were
the worst, gettin' to know each other, like. We had
a couple of cross words *then*. Mick's not much of a
talker," he added, sighing heavily.

"Really," said Jimmy.

"Plus," Stump continued, unabashed, "you
wouldn't believe how many people just walk right by,
don't even lift a finger when they hear a bloke in distress; ain't that right, Mick? Bloody scoutmasters."

Jimmy frowned. "Scoutmasters?"

"Yeah," said Stump reasonably. "At any rate, he
looked like a scoutmaster. He had a lot of kids with
him, didn't he, Mick?"

Back in Dullitch, the city's fragile morale was beginning
to crack.

"I'm sorry, the *what*?" Duke Modeset asked, leaning across his desk and cupping a hand to his ear.

"The, er, the Dullitch Society for the Successful Location and Safe Return of Missing Children, milord," said Pegrand.

"And they're demanding my abdication?"

"Yes, milord."

"Nonsense!" exclaimed Modeset. "I've never even heard of them. In fact, I'd be surprised if they existed before lunch."

Pegrand smiled nervously. "They say they've been going twenty years, milord. You know, on the off-chance."

"Ah yes, like the Association for Making Friends with the People of Phlegm Before They Invade Us Next Tuesday? Or even, what was it, the Long-Established League Against the Early Closing of the Rotting Ferret on a Friday Night? Ha! They must think I was born upside down in a haystack. Tell them to drop dead."

"Yes, milord," said Pegrand.

"But not in those words, of course."

"'Course not, milord." Pegrand shuffled some documents and, holding them out to the duke, he continued, "They did have this, though."

Modeset sighed and rubbed his eyelids. "What is it?"

"Er, well, it's a petition demanding answers, milord."

"Is it signed?" asked Modeset.

"Yes, milord."

"Just the one page?"

"Er, yes, milord. Oh, no, tell a lie, there're two. Unless this one's part . . . oh right, three. Oh, no, four . . . and the two I've just dropped."

"Give it to me!"

Modeset reached up, snatched the sheaf of documents and threw them straight into the bin.

"Now, go and find Quaris Sands!" he snapped. "We need a workable speech by the morning and I'm damn sure I'm not going to be the one writing it."

SEVENTEEN

JIMMY was trying to get a grip on his excitement.

"Let me get this straight," he said. "You saw a stranger leading a large group of children through here?"

"Yeah, like I said," Stump yawned. "There's a grate in the back of the cell, you see. I saw 'em all filing past in the next tunnel, so I shouted for help. Funny thing was, they didn't even hear me! It was like they were all hypnotized or somethin'. Totally zonked. Are you all right? You look like you've seen a ghost."

Jimmy swallowed, swallowed, and swallowed again. "Please listen to me very carefully," he began, his hands shaking violently as he spoke. "My name is Jimmy Quickstint; I come from Dullitch. That scout-master is some kind of evil enchanter. He *stole* those children from Dullitch, and I need to get them back before, well, before he decides to do something unspeakable to them."

"That's awful!" Stump gasped. "Hang on, though, wait a minute; are you telling me they've sent you out on your own to stop this fella?"

"No, not exactly. I was supposed to find these mer-cenaries who are traveling with my granddad—he's an ex-sorcerer, by the way—and oh, it's all too complicated to explain now! Listen, do you think there's any way we can get through this wall?"

Stump peered into his cell for what seemed like a long time. "No," he said eventually, turning back. "But you shouldn't need to. The Twelve's full of these tunnels; one big network from the outside in; junc-tions all over the place. You just have to follow this tunnel through; no doubts it'll link up to the others somewhere along the line. Maybe Mick would know, he's lived down here for years."

This time, Jimmy just couldn't let the question go unspoken.

"Is Mick a ghost?" he asked tentatively.

Stump frowned at him. "Mick doesn't know whether to be insulted or not by that remark."

"Oh, sorry. Tell him I apologize."

"Look," said Stump, suddenly straightening up. "I ain't no mediator; tell him yourself."

"I can't see him!" shouted Jimmy. He shoved the prisoner aside, marched into the cell and walked twice around it. Then he got down on his hands and knees to crawl under a sloping wall in the rear of the room. Stump watched with a detached amusement.

"What are you up to?" he asked.

"I'm just trying to prove to myself," said Jimmy, prodding a leg into parts the rest of him couldn't reach, "that I'm not going crazy. There is no Mick."

"Did you hear that, Mick?" said Stump. "He says you don't exist."

The thief struggled to his feet and shook his head. Of all the prisoners in all the cells, in all the lands, he thought, why did I have to get this lunatic?

Then he saw Mick waving at him.

Standing on the prisoner's palm was a man two inches tall. He was wearing britches and a jerkin. He had a tiny eye patch over one eye. Jimmy gaped at him.

"See?" said Stump, excitedly. "That's Mick, that is."

"Flimder," said Mick. It sounded more like a squeak than a word.

"What is he?" Jimmy asked, fascinated.

"Mick's a mite. Says he's the bastard son of Tim Index. He don't say much, but I think we understand each other on a kind of spiritual level. He might be telepathic."

The little man produced a miniature rope and looped the end over Stump's forefinger. Then he started to rappel down the prisoner's hand.

"Look at him," said Stump cheerfully. "He's always tryin' to get away."

Jimmy watched as he flicked his wrist and caught the mite back in the palm of his hand.

"He's a real one for escaping, is Mick."

"But that's ridiculous! He could've walked between the bars at any time."

"Eh?"

Jimmy shook his head in disbelief. "You said," he began, trying to speak in plain language in case Stump was having problems in that department, "that he was already here when you arrived. Why didn't he just leave?"

"I think he'd made himself at home, to be honest. He had a nice little house built out of an old tinderbox."

"What happened to that?" said Jimmy, looking around again.

"I landed on it."

"Flimder," said Mick, shaking a minuscule fist at the prisoner. It appeared to be the only sound the little creature was capable of making.

"You know something, Stump?" said Jimmy.

"What's that?"

"I don't think Mick likes you very much."

Jimmy slumped down on to the dusty stone and wiped some sweat from his forehead with the back of his hand.

"So," he said. "We know the children are down here somewhere. If we find them, that leaves me to fight the enchanter. Great, just great. I wonder where Granddad is?"

Groan Teethgrit was experiencing a situation which, to his mind, simply didn't add up. Usually when he threw punches people fell; most times they just fell over and, occasionally, they fell thousands of feet. They never just stood there looking at him. Groan felt as if he were punching a cushion.

The giant just stood motionless, and continued to glare.

"C'mon then," Groan managed, after the third blow had failed to garner a reaction. "I'm not touchin' me sword, this is fightin' ol' style, han' to han'. Lesee what you got."

The giant reeled back and gave him a slap. Groan sailed backward, hitting a young coomba tree so hard that he actually heard the roots splitting as he lost consciousness.

The giant stepped amid the rubble and reached down to pick up the comatose barbarian. Unexpectedly, he got a battle-axe buried in his back. It felt like a wasp sting.

Gordo yanked as hard as could but the axe simply wouldn't come loose. He put one foot on the giant's back for leverage and found himself on the receiving end of a slap from a hand of pumpkin proportions. The giant didn't see where Gordo landed, but he did see, out of the corner of his eye, the old man running toward him, frantically waving a broken branch. He stretched out a fist and there was a dull thud. The branch fell to the floor.

The giant yawned, removed the axe from his back, and hung it on a belt hook. Then he slung Tambor over one shoulder, snatched hold of Groan's boots, and began dragging the barbarian back through the forest. On the way, he collected Gordo Goldeaxe, who'd landed upside down in a briar patch.

In the far distance, a coil of smoke headed skyward. The giant smiled. He always lit a succession of small fires whenever he went out to chop wood. They marked the path back to the entrance of his cave in the mountainside. He headed toward it with his new prisoners, feeling that on the whole, life couldn't get much better.

EIGHTEEN

S TUMP had secreted Mick about his person.
Jimmy didn't dare to ask where.

This is ridiculous, he thought. Even if I do find
out where the foreigner took them, how am I ever
going to sneak hundreds of children out of a mountain without him noticing?

"Look," he said eventually, employing what he
hoped was a friendly smile. "I've got to start looking.
Can you help me?"

"No," answered Stump, flatly.

Jimmy boggled at him. "No? You won't help me rescue kidnapped children?"

"The thing is," Stump continued, "it feels like I've been down here for ages and I wanna go back and see my family, you know how it is. Beryl, that's my wife, she's probably remarried, thinkin' I'm a goner."

"Oh, right," said Jimmy. "You'd better get back to her, then."

"Yeah, well, you know how it is. Sorry about that; good luck and all."

"Thanks. I think."

Jimmy nodded, got to his feet and marched off toward the lower staircase.

"No hard feelings," Stump called after him. "I'm sure you aaaahhh! Mick! Stop bitin' me!"

"Tambor?"

Eyelids flickered. A light in the darkness: small, indistinct. It hovered around at the edge of the sorcerer's field of vision. Then, slowly, shapes began to swim into focus. He saw a lot of faces, no, correction; he saw a lot of *face*. . . .

"You're all right, then?" asked Gordo.

"Let's not jump to any conclusions," said Tambor weakly.

"I thought you might be dead," said Gordo.

Tambor stared blearily around the room. It seemed to be a cell of some kind. He noted the half-rusted chains and manacles that hung from every wall. A tiny grille offered one of only two light sources, the other being a rather pathetic candle, half melted, on a shelf above Gordo's head. There were also some half-rotted torches stacked in one corner.

The dwarf was kneeling beside him. Blood leaked from a cut on his forehead and his clothes were in tatters. Despite all this, he seemed as companionable as ever. Groan was lying flat out like a felled oak. He twitched every few seconds.

The sorcerer moaned. A dull throb that had started in the base of his spine was gradually working its way north, planning a terrible assault on his neck and shoulders. "What happened?" Tambor said.

"Well, I don't know what happened to you, but we've taken a right old belting. Groan got KO'd by the giant, and I tried to help but he knocked me flying. Then I think he must have dragged us up to his cave. Groan was spark out, but I came round pretty quick." Gordo grinned with masculine pride. "I'm tougher than I look."

"You'd have to be. So, in fact, we're inside a cell, inside the giant's cave, inside the mountain. Sound right?"

"Yep, that's the way of it."

"I don't understand," said Tambor. "Why would he keep us here?"

"Who knows?" answered Gordo. "Maybe he'll ransom us."

Tambor nodded, and had a good go at a positively wretched expression. As his vision improved, so the scene around him was becoming progressively worse. When things were bad they were bad; you didn't want details.

For example, he hadn't seen the snake before. It slithered from a hole in the wall and wriggled into a crevice beneath the stone staircase. A number of indescribable obscenities crawled, on a wide variety of legs, across the cell floor. Tambor closed his eyes and pretended he was somewhere sunny.

There was a commotion outside, the cell door flew open and a few plates were thrown in, landing facedown on the stone. The door closed again.

Tambor managed to fight off a few of the milder monstrosities to gain possession of something that looked like a distant relation to the dumpling.

He bit hard, closed his eyes, and swallowed. "I expect he's fattening us up," he told Gordo. "Well, fattening two of us up. He might want to starve you."

"He'd better not," snapped the dwarf. "Before we got into this mess, I hadn't missed a single meal in thirty years."

"Now, why don't I find that surprising?" said Tambor sarcastically.

He struggled to his feet and kicked some dust over a dubious shadow in the corner. When it didn't slink back or make a dive for his leg, he gave it a tentative tap with the toe of his boot. It turned out to be an old rag. He subjected it to a malicious stare, and then kicked some more dust over it. "Well, we're done for, then," he said.

Gordo gazed up at him, his face radiating surprise. "Really?" he said. "I was sure you'd think of something. You sorcerers always struck me as the intelligent sort, specially when it comes to escape and the like."

"Oh, we are, generally speaking," said Tambor. "It's just that, well, being a sorcerer with a bad memory and no spell book doesn't really prepare you for a prison break, if you know what I mean."

"Mmm. I see your point," said Gordo. "So, that's it. We're doomed."

"So it would appear," said Tambor, with a sigh.

They sat sharing the embarrassed silence for a while, before Gordo jumped to his feet. "I've got an idea," he said.

Tambor started; he'd seen ideas dawn on people before, but Gordo gave the term "stroke of genius" a literal meaning.

"Why don't we turn out our pockets and see if we've

got anything that might get us out?" he said, excitedly.

"Fine," said Tambor. "Let's see. I've got a mouse-trap and a piece of cheese. How about you?"

"Er, oh . . . I don't have anything. Sorry."

"Good plan, though."

"Thanks," said Gordo.

"I'm going to sleep now," said Tambor, yawning. "Wake me up if anything dramatic happens."

Jimmy had been wandering along the same dank tunnel for what seemed like hours. He looked at the walls on either side of him, wondering if it was one of those deceptive tunnels, where it appeared as if you were getting somewhere when you were actually just walking around in a circle.

It was gloomy too; secret tunnels and passageways beneath a mountain should surely be covered in symbols and runes or something. Not like this one, all brown and sewery. He reached out and touched a wall that felt pretty much the same as the walls back home.

Jimmy was just wondering whether he should check for hidden doors or concealed levers, when he heard footsteps approaching. He panicked and ran along the passage a little way, his head throbbing as he searched for somewhere to hide. There was nowhere. How could you hide in a place like this? He realized that the only way to survive would probably be to surprise whoever it was, and the only way he could do that would be to lie down on the floor and suddenly leap up, before he was trodden on. Things didn't go according to plan.

"Ahh! My nose—"

"Sorry, mate."

Jimmy looked up and could just about make out a grubby countenance staring down at him. "Stump?" he managed. "I thought you'd gone."

"Couldn't get past the rock door," said the prisoner, looking around the tunnel with a grim smile.

"No, I tried getting back out that way when I first came in," said Jimmy.

"Sick and tired of this place," sighed Stump.

"I'm not surprised. Good of you to come back, anyway. Even though you didn't have any option."

"Exactly," said Stump. "So, how are you gettin' on? Found the children yet, have you?"

Jimmy subjected him to a thoughtful look. "Do you see any children?"

The prisoner peered over his shoulder and shook his head.

"Well, then," said Jimmy. "Let's assume the obvious, shall we?"

Stump reached down to pick some grime from his

toenails. "Pity about Mick," he said, after a while. "I really liked him."

"Why?" asked Jimmy. "What happened?"

"Well, I thought if Mick crawled through that little gap beside the slab he could probably get us some help."

"And?" Jimmy prompted.

"The slab must not have shut properly. It rolled over a bit more."

"That's terrible!" said Jimmy, shaking his head. "Poor Mick."

"I know," Stump agreed. "You thought he was small before, you should see him now."

Jimmy suddenly put a finger to his lips. "Did you hear that?" he said. "Sounds like . . . I don't know, like *something.*"

Stump paused for a second, head on one side, and then shrugged.

"Nah," he said. "It's this place, ain't it? Gets to you after a while."

"I'm sure I heard something," Jimmy insisted.

"Could be goblins. You get a lot of goblins in places like this."

Jimmy nodded. He wondered briefly about the rat purge in Dullitch. Perhaps the foreigner hadn't drowned them after all, he thought. Maybe he had brought them here.

"Allo allo allo," said Stump, who was prodding the floor with his foot. "What's all this, then?"

Jimmy looked over his shoulder. "Have you found something?" he asked.

"Yeah, a thingy on the floor," Stump answered. "It feels like a pedal or somethin'." He smiled. "Reckon I should push it?"

"Don't you?" said Jimmy.

"I'm not too lucky with these things. Last time I pushed a pedal in the dark, I spent six months in a scorpion pit."

"How did you get out of that one?" Jimmy asked.

"Leather soles."

"Wow."

"Damn right." He checked the pedal again. "So, do you reckon I should step on it or not?"

Jimmy looked both ways and shrugged. "You might as well," he said. "We're not getting anywhere, here."

"What're you doing?" said Tambor.

"Well, the giant didn't take my axe away, did he?" said Gordo. "Or Groan's sword. Why was that, d'you think?"

Tambor remained silent.

"Humiliation point, isn't it?" said Gordo. "He's showin' us we can't take him out even when we're armed."

Tambor nodded. "I see, so you're . . ."

"I'm just making the best of a bad situation," said Gordo. He was scraping away at the wall with the head of his battle-axe. A few grains of dust drifted down from the brickwork.

"You'll never get out of a cell like that," said Tambor, shaking his head. "People escaping from prisons by scraping away a bit at a time, it's all just stories. It doesn't actually work. Besides, how do you know this is his cave? He could've taken us to some sort of giant fortress. You could just be scraping your way into the next cell."

Gordo stopped scraping, turned and gave the sorcerer a wry smile.

"Can you feel it?" he said.

"Feel what?" asked Tambor.

"There's a draft coming from this wall. There's probably a long abandoned passageway behind it."

"Or a lot of people blowing," said Tambor, who knew the way the gods worked.

"*Grphnu,*" said Groan. He forced himself up onto his elbows. "Where am I?"

"In the infamous cell of a thousand secret exits," said the sorcerer sarcastically.

"What hit me?" asked Groan, groggily.

"Same thing that hit me," Gordo muttered.

"Here," said the barbarian, struggling to his feet and marching over to Gordo. "Don't bovva wiv that."

There was a low rumble and a section of tunnel slid away.

"Well, look at that," said Stump, standing back.

Jimmy stepped inside. The new tunnel was considerably brighter than the one they had been traveling along. It looked as if it might actually lead somewhere.

NINETEEN

SOMEWHERE in the darkness, a wall heaved.

Behind the wall, various nocturnals scurried away.

A second concrete belch rocked the tunnel, larger this time, more weight behind it.

Then the wall crashed down.

"'S dark," said Groan, widening the gap in the cell wall by booting out a few rogue bricks around the edge. "You got any good torch spells, sorcerer?"

Tambor nodded and tried to think of the one that was hovering on the edge of his memory. It was a good torch spell, and, best of all, it didn't require fire pel-lets. What it *did* require was a torch, but he'd snatched one of those from the cell and had it stashed inside his robe. Still, he supposed, there was no point in bring-ing it out if he couldn't light it.

"Bloke who sold me this battle-axe," said Gordo, "told me it could glow in the dark."

One after another, they stepped into the passage-way. Groan blocked the opening so that they could test out Gordo's "torch."

It was pitch-dark in the tunnel.

Nothing happened.

At length, Tambor turned to the dwarf. "Was there a low counter in the shop?" he said.

Gordo shrugged. "Why?"

"I'm just wondering how that shopkeeper managed to see you coming."

Groan was first to laugh at the joke, which had a lot to do with there being three of them, and both of the others were involved in the telling. "P'raps if we follow this tunnel it might lead somewhere," he said, once he'd stopped chuckling.

"You reckon?" said Gordo, praying for strength.

They walked along in single file, Gordo leading and Groan bringing up the rear. Tambor stumbled back and forth between them.

Suddenly, a torch struck up in the darkness, bathing the tunnel in a warm glow.

Groan and Gordo started.

"Where did you get that?" said the dwarf.

Tambor's grin was so wide that it looked as if his face had split. "In the prison," he said. "I just wanted to get it alight before I gave it to you." He passed the torch to Groan and the party continued forward.

"So the old magic's coming back to your fingertips is it?" said Gordo.

"Hah! I'm as surprised as you are. Isn't it fantastic? Memory's a wonderful thing, you know. The Naked Flame was one of the three spells I learned in my first week at the Elistalis in Dullitch. They've all but demolished the old academy now, you know."

Gordo nodded; he'd recalled the building on his first visit to the city. It had been a sight to behold, with its gleaming silver walls and the giant metal rings that spun endlessly on the roof. "Shame about that. It was very, er, dominating."

"What were the uvver two spells?" asked Groan, who was forever destined to remain half a conversation behind.

"Well," Tambor began, biting his bottom lip. "There was the Tower of Screaming Doom, but, of course, you've seen that." He ignored Gordo's loud sniggering. "And then there was *Mortis Portalitas*."

"What's that?" asked Gordo.

"The Door of Death. That is, the opening of an interdimensional portal between this realm and limbo."

"You were taught that on your first day?"

"No, I said I *learned* it on my first day," answered Tambor. "In actual fact, I read in on the wall in the boys' latrine."

"Stone me. Don't be in too much of a hurry to remember that one, will you?" said Gordo.

"Hah! I've practiced, of course, but I've never had the nerve to actually finish the summoning."

A little way down the tunnel Tambor noticed a small square of indentations on what he took to be the east wall. He squinted at it. The patch consisted mostly of rough lines pulled together to make a language that didn't quite sit right, no matter how you read it. It seemed as if who- ever had made the markings hadn't known how to spell the longer words properly and, instead of checking things through, had just taken his chances.

"What is it?" said Gordo. He'd walked another twenty odd yards down the tunnel alone and was pretty annoyed that no one had bothered to call him back. Groan said nothing.

"It's some sort of writing. Hold on, I'm trying to

translate. I think it's religious," said Tambor, feeling along the scratches with his index finger.

"Mmm," he said, after a time. "It says that in the beginning there was a stick."

"What kind of stick?" said Gordo. "Did it have things coming out of it?"

"Just says a stick," Tambor answered.

"Was it one o' them sticks wiv' two ends?" said Groan, deep in thought.

"I don't know, it doesn't seem that important. Either that or there was a loss of concentration, because then it starts going on about a garden." Tambor leaned closer.

"'And the gods said, Eat of any tree in the garden, but be very careful that it be from the garden and not from anywhere else because'"—Tambor paused to catch his breath—"'just outside the garden lives a serpent who makes his own fruit with instruments we didn't give him.'"

"Are you sure this is authentic?" asked Gordo, frowning.

Tambor shrugged.

"How does it finish, then?" said Groan, who was getting restless.

"Er, let me see. . . . Oh, here, there's a prediction about the end of the world."

"Bet magic causes it," Groan said, as he spat on the floor.

"Don't be stupid," Tambor snapped. "Magic is perfectly safe in the right hands." He went on to read about an old mage who wrote a magic book that led to the collapse of what, on Illmoor, would have passed for civilized society.

"It reckons a barbarian invasion will thrust the world back into the dark age," Tambor lied.

"I thought we were in that already," said Gordo, thoughtfully.

"It's all rubbish anyway, apart from the last bit," said Tambor.

"Why, what does that say?"

Tambor squinted. "Well, apparently, we're inside the Twelve, and it's a warning. It advises us not to venture any farther unless we want to end up lost for the rest of eternity in a terrible labyrinthine maze."

"Hah! Load o' junk. C'mon, let's move," said Groan.

They continued along the tunnel, which sloped down for a few yards and then veered sharply to the right.

"Here," said the dwarf, suddenly stopping. Tambor practically tumbled over him.

"What is it?" asked Groan.

Gordo knelt down and ran his hand over the

ground. He checked and double-checked, then reached a conclusion. "It's a grate," he said. "In the floor."

"Can you lift it?" Tambor inquired, hopefully.

"Think so. Only one way to find out, eh?"

There followed a moment of frantic fumbling and a few mild curses when a finger got trapped. Then a scratching ensued, which turned into a shaking and ended in a mad hammering. Tambor felt a chill sneak inside his robe. It started to give his legs a hard time. He felt ancient goose bumps begin to resurface.

"Hang on a minute," said Gordo, finally. He was still down on his knees, but had apparently stopped trying to force the grate. "It's massive." He peered back along the floor of the tunnel. "Groan, I reckon you're even standing on it."

The barbarian tried to look under him and, failing to see anything, stamped his foot. There was an expansive creak.

"No-o-o-o-o!" screamed Tambor, but it was too late.

The grate fell away and the trio plummeted through the floor. Groan snatched at a broken rung, but he couldn't hold on to it. The torch Tambor had been clutching teetered on the edge of the grate, flickered, and went out.

❊ ❊ ❊

"I've seen these before," said Stump, looking down at a floor covered with mosaic tiles. The room seemed completely out of character against the background of the dungeon passageway. Jimmy had never seen so many bright colors, and it was extraordinarily well lit with braziers. He wondered if the gods employed a caretaker; there were certainly some very big foot-prints nearer the wall.

"So what's it all about?" Jimmy asked.

"Well," said Stump, crouching down. "You got to step on the right ones. If you don't you gets an arrow flying at you from them holes in the wall, there. See?"

Jimmy saw the circles and nodded. They were tiny. He shuddered. Arrows that small could probably shoot right through you and you wouldn't feel it until all your bits ran out of juice.

Stump was preparing to demonstrate. He reached out and brushed a finger along the surface of the first tile. Nothing happened. He went through the same procedure with the tile next to it, and got a similar response.

"Oh, well," he said, after carrying out a spot check on a further seven surfaces. "Maybe they're all spent or something."

Jimmy smiled as the prisoner got up, walked into

the center of the room and collapsed with an arrow in his leg. Three more shot from the holes over his head. Stump was writhing on the mosaic tiles.

"Hold on!" Jimmy called. "I'm coming over."

He dropped onto his stomach and began to pull himself toward the injured prisoner. Arrow traps exploded above him, but he reached his companion with little difficulty.

"I'm gonna pass out," said Stump, eyes fluttering.

"Don't be ridiculous. Actually, you're very lucky; it didn't bite that far into your flesh," said Jimmy, examining Stump's wound.

"Oh great! Thank the lords for small mercies. If I wasn't *aaahhhhh!*"

Jimmy yanked the dart from Stump's leg, tossed it aside, tore off a scrap of his jerkin, and dabbed away the blood.

"There you go," he said, smiling.

"I'm gonna pass out," said Stump.

"But it only bled a gnat's wing!" shouted Jimmy. "You lost about a thimbleful."

"It don't matter," said Stump. "I can't afford to lose any. Look at the size of me."

Jimmy shook his head in amazement and crawled to the edge of the mosaic floor, dragging the injured prisoner after him.

✷ ✷ ✷

"Where are we, then?" said Groan, rolling over onto his back and staring at the ceiling.

Gordo coughed. "Hell?" he ventured.

"I can't see a thing," said Tambor. "I'm going to crawl over this way a bit. Tell me if I bump into you."

"You'll know if you bump into Groan," said the dwarf.

"Of course, sorry. It's the dungeon, it warps your *mi–i–i–i–i–i–i. . . .*"

There was silence.

"Tambor?" said Gordo, listening intently.

Nothing.

"Groan?"

"Yeah?"

"What happened to Tambor?"

"Dunno," answered Groan. "I don't fink he's 'ere anymore."

The dwarf crawled around in the dark. He sounded like a pig sniffing out truffles.

"Hold on a minute," said Gordo, finally. "There's some sort of *ahhhhhh!*"

Groan got to his feet in the darkness.

"What's this, hide-'n'-seek?" he muttered, testily.

He padded around the room, his back against the wall. When he had circled it entirely, he stepped in a little and tried again. His foot caught the edge of something smooth and sloping. He dropped down onto one knee and felt it with his hands. It was a chute of some kind.

"Oi!" he shouted down it. "You all right down there?"

There was no reply.

"All right," Groan boomed. "I'm comin' down."

Jimmy grabbed hold of Stump's arm and pulled him back. They were about fifty yards beyond the arrow-trap room.

"Now, don't tell me you can't hear *that*," said Jimmy.

Stump put his head on one side. "Yeah, I can."

"What do you think it is?" asked Jimmy.

"Could be up on the mountain or somethin'," Stump suggested.

"No. It's closer than that. Listen carefully," Jimmy whispered.

"P'raps there's a tunnel above us?"

"Could be," said Jimmy. "That's definitely voices, though. Don't you think?"

"Sounds like shoutin' to me, people shoutin' somethin'."

"Listen," Jimmy interrupted. "It's getting nearer."

"Hey," said Stump, pointing toward the roof of the tunnel. "There's a huge great hole in the ceiling."

Jimmy looked up.

His granddad fell on him. For a second they both just lay there, frozen with shock. Then a dwarf cannoned through the same hole and landed on top of them.

Stump whistled between his teeth and shook his head.

"Blimey," he said. "I'm glad I weren't standin' there."

Then Groan arrived.

TWENTY

IT WAS EARLY morning in Dullitch and there was already a fair turnout for the big speech. Many of the citizens felt aggrieved at the prospect of having to endure life without their children. A few of them had come to give thanks.

The weather was surprisingly benevolent, smothering the landscape with warm sunlight, while at the same time cooling it with gentle breezes. It was looking to become one of those rare days where people whistled on their way home from work and birds twittered merrily from the

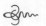

rooftops. At around noon, picnics began to dot the lower reaches of Skulkis, transforming the tor into a patchwork of white and green—a chessboard with brightly colored pawns. Things soon went downhill as the city's indefatigable inhabitants began to steal from each other's baskets but, for the moment at least, all was peaceful.

In the palace, Quaris Sands was writing a speech. He was aided in the task by Duke Modeset and the troglodyte, Burnie (the only other member of the council who'd agreed to come along). Luckily, the conference room was at the top of the tallest tower and the occasional screams of the crowd were barely audible.

"There you are, milord," said the acting chairman. He applied the final full stop and passed the speech across to Modeset, who read a few lines in each paragraph before crossing them through and scribbling over the top of them.

"Um, which bits are you changing, milord?" asked Quaris, trying to ignore the glob of green slime which had just missed the back of his hand. He threw a stern look in Burnie's direction.

"Any bits with us mentioned negatively," Modeset replied, indicating half the page. "I'm not sure that a fair proportion of the blame cannot be assigned to our friend Quarry," said Modeset with a smile. "He has the look of a culprit. Any chance of rewording the speech so that most of the responsibility lies with him?"

Three floors below the conference room, Pegrand Marshall was attempting to get a squommet out of its basket. He sat down cross-legged before the little creature, whistled between his teeth, and waved a biscuit hopefully. "Fizz! C'mon, Fizz, out you come."

The shape remained dormant.

Squommets were a peculiar species, a one-winged dragon-beaver. They were incredibly furry, with large teeth that extended from the base of their mouths in a sharp curve over their top lip. Fizz had been Pegrand's pet for two days and was, he had to admit, a poor example of the species. He'd bought it from a well-renowned sanctuary in Plum Hill. They had assured him of its good line, which just goes to show that excessive inbreeding can corrupt the good genes in any species. He'd even been shown a portrait of Fizz's parents, taken outside a hostelry near the almshouses. He looked down into the basket. Perhaps he's adopted, Pegrand thought.

Fizz stretched out a claw, tentatively at first. Then he hopped out of the basket and wiggled across the floor. Pegrand reached down, scooped him up in his arms, and went back to the basket. As usual, Fizz's paper needed changing. Pegrand lowered himself onto his haunches and picked up the dirty sheet. He was about to throw it away, when he noticed there was some scribbled-out writing on it which he could just about make out. It was a letter:

MaRicus DArk, AssaSSiN
HOusE oF the Rooftop RUnNers
6 PAlACE STrEet
DuLLiTch

DEarest FriEnd,
    I WoNdEr if You CouLd bE so Kind As to hElP
Me at this tiME. How long hAve wE bEen
friEnds? I WISh for You to aRRaNGe A Sma

The rest of the message was either crossed through or illegible. Pegrand held it up to the light, but still couldn't make out the signature. Then he toyed with it pensively, running over a number of possibilities in his head. One kept recurring. He tossed Fizz roughly back into the basket, pocketed the paper, and bolted off toward the kitchens.

From his vantage point atop Karuim's Church of Holy Origins, the assassin Mifkindle Green loaded his patented silver crossbow, leaned over the shoulders of two conveniently positioned gargoyles, and peered along the shaft at his target. There was a procession going on. This was nothing unusual; there was always a procession going on in Dullitch. A big speech was about to be made, an explanation to be given.

The gathering below had attracted a large percentage of the city, which was no surprise. Among the throngs of noblemen, merchants, and market traders, Mifkindle had already spotted Lord Bancroft, Baron Richford, and Lady Terps of Pullville. He wasn't interested in any of these, however. His particular target was Duke Modeset, a man who seemed to be single-handedly responsible for the current collapse of society. Mifkindle checked to ensure that the bolt was loaded before peering across at the opposite roof, to ensure that his position was being monitored by a Runners representative. The monitor waved back at him.

"Think carefully," Pegrand urged the maid.

She'd been steadily shaking her head for the best part of ten minutes. "I know I went up to the dining room and out to the stables," she said, nervously. "And then I went into town and came back and then I laid some new paper for your baby squommet but—oh yes—I went up to see Chancellor Quarry. He had some rubbish, I think. He's pretty scared, you know. I mean, what with the—where are you going?"

"Assassination attempt, milord!"

Modeset turned just in time to avoid Pegrand running into him. "I beg your pardon?" he said, quickly sidestepping the manservant.

"Assassination attempt. I believe I have been fortunate enough to happen upon a copy of a letter sent to Maricus Dark, of the Rooftop Runners assassin network. I believe they intend to pop you off during your speech, milord."

"I see," said Modeset. "Lucky for me. Any suggestions for a counterattack?"

"Don't know, milord."

Burnie sniffed, which didn't seem to clear anything. "Do the people know where you'll be coming out?" he asked.

Modeset nodded.

"Everyone's been told where to stand," said Pegrand.

"Right," said the troglodyte, cracking a knuckle somewhere in its foot. "Then I suggest you be announced."

"Sorry?" said Modeset, leaning toward him.

"I suggest you be announced to the crowd," he repeated.

"Who by?"

"I've got a suggestion, milord," said Pegrand.

Fire first and ask questions later. The assassin had to admit it was a pretty lame phrase, taken at face value; but it was the only phrase by which assassins lived. Ask questions in this business and you ended up getting your answers through the wrong end of an arrow. He peered along the crossbar and took aim.

"I assure you I—"

"Just get out there," snapped Pegrand, shoving the chancellor in the small of the back.

"But I—"

"NOW!"

Quarry stepped out onto the central balcony of Dullitch Palace. The crowd jeered in unison and began to pelt him with rotten fruit and vegetables. Unfortunately none of them found their target. But an arrow did.

The crowd lapsed into silence. A woman screamed. Quarry stared down at the ocean of faces and then up at his executioner, clutching at the arrow in his chest. Then he stumbled forward, tumbled over the balcony, and fell into the crowd.

The assassin's face became a mask of fascinated horror and he flashed a quick glance across the rooftops at his colleague, whose instinctive reaction had been to dash off toward the stairwell. He froze with fear. No assassin in his right mind would ever kill Chancellor Quarry. The man was rumored to be a high-ranking Yowler; the repercussions would be enormous! Even in the best-case scenario, he'd be facing instant dismissal.

The assassin shook his head, looked down and saw the guards. They were pouring into both the temple entrance and the entrance to the town hall across the street. He swept up his crossbow and ran.

TWENTY-ONE

"CITIZENS OF DULLITCH!" exclaimed Duke Modeset, emerging out onto the balcony to address a stunned crowd. Pegrand was holding a shield over his head. "I, your duke, and the honorary members of your city council, have come up with a solution to the peril that darkens our day. We have dispatched a hunting party to find your stolen children and bring the terrible fiend who abducted them to justice. I'd just like to point out that Mr. Quarry, your honorable ex-chancellor, has been entirely ineffectual throughout these distressing times, a fact of which our city's *magnificent* assassins were evidently aware."

He looked down and smiled at the citizens of Dullitch. They were disposing of the late chancellor by passing his body over their heads. Modeset noticed that a funeral cart had pulled up at the back of the crowd. Was it his imagination, he wondered, or did it arrive before the chancellor landed?

"Oi, mister!"

The cry rang out like the call of a highly strung bird. Duke Modeset peered down as the crowd parted for a small boy with a smudge of brown hair. Supported on a wooden crutch, he had one leg, and that distinctive look mastered by the downtrodden.

"Yes, young man?" said the duke, smiling.

"I reckon it was you what was responsible for the ratcatcher. I 'eard you didn't pay 'im nuffin' for drownin' all o' them rats."

"I see. And you are?"

"Tom Piddleton!" answered the boy. "I'm the orphan what escaped the evil clutches of the music man!"

"Yes, that's right: so I heard. Very convenient, wasn't it?"

The crowd, which had been about to erupt, went suddenly silent.

"Do what, mister?" asked the boy.

"I said it was very convenient—you getting away so easily," sneered the duke.

"Eh? I couldn't keep up. That music man, he waved his arms an' made all the other kids float on air. I was too far back, I don't think he even saw me."

"Oh, is that right? Of course he didn't *see* you. After all, I'm certain he wouldn't have spared you your freedom out of pity. Not after leading all of our children to their certain dea—detainment. Isn't it more likely that he *did* see you lagging behind and decided to allow you to stagger home just so you could inform the populace of his powers and, in doing so, insight a riot? Isn't this the case? *Isn't it so?*" demanded the duke.

The crowd looked unsure, but it was wavering.

"I put it to you," Modeset continued, his glare intensifying with the pitch of his voice, "that you are nothing more than a consort of 'the music man,' a *hireling* returned to the city to cause civic unrest. Well, it won't work, you hear me? The good folk of Dullitch can see through such scams! I will let them judge you! Hahahahahahaha!"

Modeset flung his arms, dark lord—like, into the air and watched with unconcealed glee as the naive majority of the crowd closed in on little Tommy Piddleton.

Behind the palace balcony, Burnie and Quaris Sands shared a worried frown.

After the crowd had dispersed (or, rather, after they had gathered into small groups to discuss various strikes and protests), Modeset and Pegrand returned to the conference room.

"Good showing out there, milord," said Quaris Sands encouragingly, shaking out his robe and taking a seat at the table.

"Meanwhile," said Burnie, "what are we going to do about the very real possibility that we've seen the last of both the mercenaries and the thief? I mean, people are bound to be up in arms before long."

"I have thought of a solution," said Modeset sternly.

"Yes, milord?"

"I suggest a concentrated diversion is in order," he said, turning to the others. "We need to take people's minds off the crisis in hand, buy ourselves some time, as it were. Therefore, I propose that we hold a fair in the palace grounds."

"A fair, milord?" asked Pegrand, doubtfully.

"Yes! You know: singing, dancing, folk music, games, etcetera. Quaris, I want you and Burnie to go to the alchemists and tell them we need to prepare a heavy-duty fireworks display. Pegrand, I want you to assemble the finest team of Morris dancers in the city. Once we've done that, maybe—"

The troglodyte tentatively raised a claw.

"Well?" asked Modeset impatiently.

"Er, sorry to interrupt, milord, but I'm thinking that the alchemists might expect some sort of payment, and what with the coffers empty and everything . . ."

"Simple." Modeset shrugged. "Tell them we're hunting for new barracks for the city militia, and their academy looks the right size. I feel certain they'll run over each other to help. Now, get to it!"

As the group scurried from the conference room, Modeset turned and crossed over to the window, scanning the closest rooftops for assassins. Evidently, the Yowlers were becoming as restless as the general populace. It wouldn't be long before they tried again. The clock was ticking.

TWENTY-TWO

"WHO'S THIS I'M ON?" said Groan, lifting his lower regions to enable the prisoner a gasp of air.

"That's Stump," said Jimmy, nervously. Gordo helped Tambor to his feet, and patted some dust from the sorcerer's shoulders as he did so.

Jimmy rubbed his shoulder. "Stump, this is my granddad," he said. "And these are, er, his friends."

"I don't got no friends," said Groan, scowling.

"I'm Gordo, this is Groan," said the dwarf, leaning against the tunnel wall.

"Never mind the introductions," snapped

Tambor. "What the devil are you doing here, lad?"

"Er, looking for you," Jimmy lied. "And the children."

"What children?" said Gordo.

"The children of Dullitch," Jimmy continued, breathlessly. "The foreigner took them when he wasn't paid for killing the rats."

Gordo frowned. "Took them?" he said. "Took them where?"

"He didn't get paid?" said Groan, who had a different set of values.

"Everyone shut up!" shouted Tambor. "Let the boy speak."

Four pairs of eyes fixed on the thief, who suddenly became quite timid.

"Er," he said, "well, when he took the children, Duke Modeset told me to come and find you and offer you a reward to get them back—"

"How much?" said Groan.

"Shhh!" said Gordo.

"I'm only askin'."

"Well don't!" the dwarf snapped. "This is serious. Being conned out of a reward is one thing, but you don't involve kiddies. That's just sick, and besides, that foreigner's not right in the head. Don't you remember when we first met him in the Ferret? His eyes were like embers and he was about ready to take on the whole bar!"

"I fort he was just daft."

Gordo shook his head. "That's not daft, that's sui-cidal. It's like he was possessed or something." He beckoned Groan over to one side. "We've got to help."

"No way," Groan said, defiantly. "We won't get paid."

"We might! Anyway, it's a matter of pride. The dwarf lords would send out an entire army if some-thing like this happened back home. I've got no love for the duke—I think he's a twisted sod—but, well, my brother's got two little ones."

"I'm not goin' 'til I see some money."

Gordo's face creased into a frown. "Fine," he said. "All these years we've known each other and it comes to this, does it? I'll go on by myself, then."

Despite the dwarf's dismissal, Groan followed him back to the group.

It was at this point that Jimmy decided, rather unwisely, to come clean about the money. "Um," he began. "The duke gave me a couple hundred crowns to give you as a down payment. The only problem is, I sort of packed them in the horse's saddlebag and it kind of, well, ran off. Your spell book was in there too, Granddad. Sorry."

Tambor rolled his eyes and was about to make a comment, when Gordo waved him into silence.

"Hang on," said the dwarf. "Let's keep focused on what's important."

"Yeah," snapped Groan. "Which way did the 'orse go?"

"What makes you think the foreigner's up here?" Gordo shouted, suddenly annoyed at his partner's single-mindedness.

"Well, *we* told him, didn't we?"

All eyes turned on Stump, who'd been waiting for an opening. "Mick and I, we saw him leadin' those kids down into the depths."

"There's got to be a path from this tunnel somewhere," said Jimmy, ignoring the fact that both Gordo and Tambor were obviously trying to look for Mick in the darkened tunnel. "All the others are just dead ends."

"Yeah," said Stump. "Besides, you don't put up a secret wall panel to hide nothin'."

Gordo shivered. "I've heard talk of this mountain," he said. "They reckon the Black Horde used to meet down here somewhere. In a great big cavern, they said."

"What Black Horde?" said Groan, who wasn't great on history.

"*The* Black Horde," said Gordo. "You know, in the old days. Those orcs that slaughtered a boatload of sorcerers from Aastenglia."

"Psst," shouted Stump, who'd ventured a little far-ther down the tunnel. "I think you should see this."

The group wandered after him, and promptly arrived at a large gate in the center of the tunnel. Beyond it lay a two-way passage, but that wasn't what the prisoner had noticed.

The dusty floor of the tunnel was covered in foot-prints, hundreds of footprints. There was also a tiny sandal just off to one side.

"Ha!" said Stump. "I told you."

TWENTY-THREE

T HE FAIR wasn't proving a total success. In fact, it had started badly and was getting worse by the minute. Currently, the duke was in the throne room, casting a cursory glance over the next phase of the entertainment.

"And here they are," said the coordinator, stepping aside and indicating the dancers with a wave of his hand. "And I'll say this: show me a better dance troupe in all the land, and you can have your money back."

Duke Modeset cast a glance over the most pathetic

assortment of miscreants he had ever set eyes on. He winced as a few of the group rushed to the aid of a member who had bent over to tie a ribbon on his leg and was having trouble standing upright again.

The duke cleared his throat. "They're all a bit, well . . . old, aren't they?" he ventured.

The coordinator shrugged. "In this case I felt only the most experienced dancers were required."

"That one at the back with no hair, milord," said Pegrand. "He's on crutches, isn't he?"

"I do believe you're right—"

"That's Mr. Cribbins," interrupted the coordinator, subjecting the duke's manservant to a malicious glare. "One of the finest clappers in the district."

Modeset gave this careful consideration. "And he's an active member of the team, is he?"

"Oh yes, certainly, without a doubt. Unless it's Folk Week, in which case he does a wonderful turn as a maypole."

There was a moment of silence.

"I think it would be fair to suggest," said Modeset evenly, "that there isn't a man in this room under seventy. Am I correct?"

The coordinator looked around, his head bobbing and weaving to achieve an all-encompassing view. "No, sir," he said eventually. "I myself am forty-seven."

Modeset pinched the bridge of his nose. "Pegrand?"

"Yes, milord?"

"Hang this man from the yardarm, will you?"

"Yes, milord. It'd be a pleasure."

Modeset dismissed the dance troupe, padded across the flagstones, and collapsed into his throne. He was suffering from a terrible headache and an impending sense of doom, but at least he still had time. Oh, sure, there were rumors of heavy vandalism downtown, but that kind of thing happened all the time—nothing to worry about. The fireworks would last for another hour, and after that, well, either the children would return or he'd be murdered by an army of marauding parents. In the event of the former, there was a slim chance that his life would be spared. A lengthy period of exile was likely, but nothing more. Modeset grimaced; his would certainly be a reign to remember. He gazed up at the portraits of his ancestors and imagined that he saw a line of mocking smiles.

He was awoken from his vision by the sound of breaking glass. Pegrand careered into the room and fell to his knees. His head was bleeding.

"We're under attack, milord," he screamed. "The palace is under attack!"

TWENTY-FOUR

THE PARTY in the cavern was watching Groan rip out an iron gate. It didn't take long; the barbarian tossed the gate aside like a child's toy. Then he marched out into the intersection, peering cautiously in both directions.

"Anything?" Gordo inquired, battle-axe at the ready.

Groan sniffed, shook his head. "Lot o' dust, nuffin much else."

Jimmy ran through the arch and knelt to study the tunnel floor. "These footsteps came from the left, so they lead down there."

The group turned to face the right-hand passage, which was blocked by a door of gargantuan proportions. Exotic-looking runes were emblazoned across its surface. They shone like gold.

"'Ere, 'old this." Groan handed Gordo his sword, then, with a running start, charged the portal. It wouldn't budge.

"What does the writin' say?" Stump asked, having second thoughts about his decision to stay in the mountain.

"It's the same language that was written on the wall," Tambor answered, a grimace forming. "It says that we're nearing a place of ancient magic, a place where terrible necromancers from the First Age went to die."

"That doesn't sound good," said Gordo.

"It's not," said Tambor. "I can't imagine that the dead rest easy in a place like this, and I have a feeling our foreigner is possessed by something raw, ancient, and extremely terrible."

"Sorcerers 're all talk," said Groan. "How 'bout the door?"

Tambor shook his head. "We'll never get through it."

"We have to!" Jimmy exclaimed. "Otherwise, the gods only know what he'll do to those children. They might be lost forever!"

"Look, I can only remember a handful of spells without a spell book!" said Tambor. "Groan can't get the door open and, with all due respect, I'm damn sure Gordo can't. What else *can* we do but—"

There was a click, and the door creaked open. Stump was standing in front of it. For a moment, the group just boggled at him. Finally, Gordo approached the scruffy prisoner. "How did you do that?" he asked, matter-of-factly.

"Er, well, I sort of turned the handle," Stump admitted. "You see, where I come from we put handles on the doors to stop people just walkin' in. Then, if you *turn* the handle like this,"—he performed a small pantomime—"the door opens. It's a proper miracle."

Gordo tried to judge whether the prisoner was being sarcastic, before deciding that, on the contrary, he was serious.

"There's a flight of stairs," Tambor said, venturing a few feet into the passage beyond. "Judging by the breeze, I'd say it probably opens into a cavern of some kind."

Jimmy snapped his fingers. "That's it," he said. "That's got to be it!"

TWENTY-FIVE

A CROWD OF ANGRY fathers stalked the streets. They'd split neatly into two groups; the vandalizers and the justice seekers.

The vandalizers consisted of those fathers who worked in the building and manual trades. In a single afternoon, they'd managed to wreck City Hall, the Treasury, and a whole host of other important civic structures.

The justice seekers, those fathers in the merchant trades who liked an ale or two, were gunning for blood.

At sunrise, they'd wanted to hurt the duke. So they demonstrated for a while, then most of them went for a small drink at the Ferret.

Lunchtime arrived, and they'd wanted to maim the duke. So they demonstrated some more, then most of them went for a small drink at the Ferret.

After lunch, they would settle for nothing less than death, but by this time they'd had rather a lot to drink; most of them knew they wanted to kill somebody, but they couldn't remember who it was.

Instead, they staggered through the streets in various stages of drunkenness, throwing stones at each other and screaming abuse. Eventually, they'd tagged along with their city-wrecking counterparts.

"Great gods," said Quaris Sands, watching from one of the only palace windows to escape the stoning. "The language! Is *scuddikuvoff* actually a word?"

Burnie shrugged, spilling something lumpy from one shoulder. "I wouldn't argue with them," he said, rolling a blobby yellow eyeball. "This is getting out of hand, though. If those children aren't found soon, there'll be nothing for them to come home to!"

"Agreed, agreed," said Quaris.

"So what are we going to do?" asked Burnie.

"I don't know! The duke's all out of ideas and I'm damn sure I am."

Quaris picked at his bushy eyebrow for a time, then appeared to reach a conclusion. "I think," he said, pausing between words for dramatic effect, "that we should climb to the top of the highest tower in the palace and jump out the window."

Burnie sighed. "Very funny. We could just hide until it all blows over."

"Hide? *Hide?* We're supposed to be in charge of the City Council!" shouted Quaris.

"Ha! Correction, beardy," said Burnie, shaking his head. "*You* are in charge of the City Council. *I* have a seat on it. Big difference. Besides, sooner or later the worst of those idiots out there are going to sober up and then they'll *really* mean business."

"But our hands are tied! We can't do anything until we've heard from the hunting party! If there even *is* a hunting party! Oh gods! Oh despair!"

Quaris grabbed two handfuls of his own hair and dropped to his knees, emitting a low, desperate moan.

Burnie watched him with a bemused smile, and said, "Any chance we think about this a bit more before you book in at the asylum?"

"It's no use. We're doomed; the children are gone, the duke is going to be murdered, the city is bankrupt, and we're all doomed!"

"Yes, fantastic; after you with the suicide pills.

However, in the meantime, we need to keep these lunatics out of the palace, so just let me think, okay?" said Burnie, pacing back and forth.

"What is there to think about? We're descending into hell," cried Quaris.

"Yes, yes. Now, pull yourself together!"

Quaris stopped moaning almost immediately, and struggled to his feet. After a few sniffles, he managed to regain some composure.

"Right," Burnie continued. "Grab some furniture and we'll try to barricade ourselves in."

"Okay, okay, but that means moving out of the shadows," said Quaris, anxiously.

The troglodyte twitched. "After you."

TWENTY-SIX

THE PARTY emerged out onto a rocky promontory overlooking a vast darkness. Jimmy was the first to get a clear view of his surroundings.

It wasn't a cavern, he decided, because caverns had roofs and this place just seemed to go on and on forever. He gazed around him in awe, feeling like a tiny insect staring up at the universe for the first time. Above, and to either side, there was darkness. Below, there were . . . children. "There they are!" Jimmy gasped, pointing downward.

The children were congregated on the cavern floor. There were hundreds of them, yet they barely made an impression on the vast expanse. Jimmy suspected that you could probably enter the cavern from the other side and walk right past them without spotting them on your way out again.

"I don't like the look of this place," said Gordo, nervously. "It's . . . distorted."

"There he is," said Tambor, pointing across the cavern.

Diek Wustapha stood atop a large boulder, surrounded by the teeming children. He was absolutely still.

"Maybe we could sneak the children out," Jimmy ventured. "There've enough caves down there. One of them must lead to the surface, law of averages. What d'you reckon? I could try it, quiet like. Besides, it doesn't look as if he's awake."

"He's awake," said Tambor, eyes narrowing. He looked down at the children who were milling around far below. They were sleepwalking, but they would only get so far before they turned back and stumbled in the opposite direction, as if repelled back toward Diek by some invisible wall of force.

"Oi!" said Groan, suddenly. "Look at 'im!"

A circle of light had formed in the air above Diek

Wustapha. It descended on him, swirling around his torso and extending outward, sweating a dark yellow light. Gordo hefted his battle-axe and took aim, but Tambor pulled him back.

"That's dark magic," he said sternly. "You've got no hope, trust me."

"What can we do, den?" said Groan, who didn't like the look of it either.

Jimmy peered over the lip of the protruding rock. It was a fair way down, he had to admit. The City Hall precipice all over again. He weighed up his chances of landing safely, then realized it probably didn't matter how he landed. If the ground didn't kill him, the foreigner would.

"I reckon I could get the children out now," he said, looking at his granddad evenly.

"I can probably help, there," said Stump, with a lopsided grin. "I'm good with kids. I've got twenty-six from my first marriage."

"Damn," said Groan and Gordo in unison, looking at the prisoner with a sudden respect.

"That leaves *us* with the foreigner," Tambor said to them, rolling up his sleeves. "Right."

Gordo noticed the old man's expression and closed a pudgy hand over his wrist. "Hold on, Tambor. What're you doing?"

"A spell."

"Not the Tower of Screaming Doom, surely?" Gordo's eyes rolled back in his head. "What good's that going to do here?"

Groan sniffed. "He might die laughin'."

The dwarf made to chuckle, but Tambor's expression stopped him dead. "I'm going to try the Doorway of Death."

"But, but . . . but you don't have your spell book!" shouted Jimmy, wide-eyed.

"I don't need it, I think I can remember," said Tambor, with a look of concentration.

"But you can't fight him with magic, Granddad. Not *him*. He's in league with something awful."

"I don't plan to *fight* him," said Tambor. "I'm going to try to open the portal behind him. I think it's just like a fissure in time. Somebody else will have to push him inside!"

"Leave that to us," Gordo said. He turned to Jimmy and Stump. "You get those kiddies out."

Jimmy nodded and peered over the edge of the promontory. Then he seemed to reach a decision. He took a few steps back, closed his eyes, and jumped. He would have landed perfectly had he remembered to open them again.

"Agggghhh—"

Tambor rushed to the edge.

"You all right?" he shouted down.

"Fine," came the reply. "Just got a bit of a pain in the *arhhhh—*"

"What?"

"It's all right. I hit my head getting up."

"Great," Gordo whispered to Groan. "If he didn't know we were here before, he knows now."

"I heard that," said Tambor, scowling at the mercenaries. "My Jimmy's a brave lad."

"Oh, he is," said Gordo, reassuringly.

It was Groan's turn to go over the edge. He unhooked a leather knapsack, which nobody had noticed before, and pulled a length of rope from inside.

"Where the hell did you get that from?" shouted Tambor.

Groan shrugged. "Always carry rope," he said. "Never know when it'll come in 'andy."

"Why didn't you say you had that before Jimmy jumped?" asked Tambor.

"You didn' ask. 'Ere, Gordo, you comin'?"

He fastened the rope around a tiny ledge above the mouth of the cave and began to rappel over the lip of the rock. The dwarf waited a while, then followed him. Stump waited in the shadows, wondering which course of action would turn out to be the best bet.

Tambor shook his head to clear his thoughts, straightened up, and returned his attention to the foreigner. Then he mumbled a few syllables and breathed a magic smoke ring through his nose. It floated in the air above him for a time, then became a thin wisp of green. Finally, it descended. As it curled around the foreigner, a strange light filled Diek's eyes.

On the ground, Gordo, Groan, and Jimmy Quickstint had stumbled upon a problem.

"It's an invisible wall," said Gordo. He took a step back and swung his battle-axe at it. There was a glancing *crack*, but nothing happened.

"Great," said Jimmy, rolling his eyes.

"Le' me 'ave a go," said Groan, putting his weight against the barrier.

"Paid good money for this axe," Gordo muttered to himself. "The bloke told me it'd go through magic barriers like a knife through butter, no problem, he said."

Groan had failed to shift the unseen boundary. Instead, he was taking out his frustration on a nearby rock.

"Maybe there's some way over it," Jimmy hazarded.

"He said to me, Gordo, why would I sell you rubbish when you're practically family, and I said—"

"Stan' back," said Groan. He picked up the rock he'd been jumping up and down on, reeled back, and hurled it at the wall. It smashed into shards.

"He's got those kids mesmerized," said Jimmy, staring into the circle. "Look at 'em. We've got to do something quick."

"_What about a dagger, the bloke said. Dwarves _should_ have a dagger, but I said—"

"Will you shut up about that stupid axe!" Jimmy screamed.

Then a bolt of energy pierced the circle. Jimmy looked up.

"It's Tambor," said Gordo, following the beam to the sorcerer's fingertips. "It must be part of the door-way spell. Why couldn't he have remembered that one when we were in the woods?"

Groan had chosen to take a running leap at the invisible barricade. This time (to his considerable sur-prise) he crashed right through it, bowling over a few of the children.

Diek Wustapha's eyes flicked open.

"He's awake!" screamed Jimmy.

The dwarf looked up. "Quick!" he shouted. "Find another exit."

All across the floor, eyes blinked and heads shook. The children were waking up. There was sobbing, crying, foul exclamations, and an awful lot of bewilderment. One or two of the more astute kids were already picking up stones as if, in true Dullitch spirit, they could smell a fight brewing.

Stump was feeling his way along the east wall of the cavern, hunting for a different set of steps. The foreigner *had* to have walked them down there somehow.

"Over there," came a shout from Jimmy. He was pointing at an arch farther along the same section of wall, a toddler clutched in his other arm. "We'll take them that way. It must join to the tunnel where they came in."

"You go on," Stump shouted. "I'm gonna see if I can find a backup route in case that one turns out to be a dead end. Be careful, though, this place is riddled with ho-o-o-o-o-o-o-o-o-oles. . . ."

Jimmy gasped; Stump had disappeared right in front of him. There was a muffled cry, becoming more distant as it progressed and, finally, it stopped. Jimmy didn't reckon he'd see Stump again.

Diek Wustapha stared blearily around the cavern. As he took stock of the situation, his eyes widened.

Interlopers: destroy them.

Stepping back on the rock, Diek raised a hand and sent a burst of green flame hurtling toward the giant barbarian.

Groan looked up just in time to avoid the blast.

Destroy him, Diek. Destroy him before he reaches you!

Diek regained his composure with a measured breath. Then he spread out his hands and a short spear materialized between them. Snatching it out of the air, Diek reached back and flung it straight at Groan, who swung out wildly with his broadsword and split the thing clean in half.

Again, Diek! Again! Give him no time to rest!

Diek acted instantaneously, driving his palm outward and producing a bolt of energy that sent Groan hurtling toward the back of the cavern. But the big barbarian was soon on his feet again, and making a determined sprint back to the center of the cavern.

Forget him, for now. Concentrate on the children.

Diek looked down at his wandering audience.

Don't let them leave, boy. Focus your mind, control them.

Diek closed his eyes and turned his palms outward. A few rogue vapors swam away on the wind, but then there was nothing. The children were no longer responding to his thoughts. He reached for the flute.

Forget that foolish toy, Diek. It's nothing; you don't need it. Watch now, see what you can do on your own. . . .

Diek gasped, and a blue mist emanated from his throat. Curling on the air, it snaked its way down toward the children and began to snare them with its tendrils, strapping arms to sides and binding feet together. Unfortunately, the strands were weak and did nothing more than hinder the children as they fought to escape.

No, no, no! If you can't manage such a simple task, then what use are you?

Diek clawed at his head, as if doing so would remove The Voice. It didn't work: if anything, the demonic tone became stronger.

What do you think you are doing? At least deal with the intruders!

Diek bit down on his lip so hard that it began to bleed. Then he cracked his knuckles, took a deep breath, and pointed his hands downward. A series of jagged blue streaks erupted from his fingertips and plunged into the cavern floor.

For a moment, nothing happened.

Then the ground started to shake.

Very well, Diek. Now you will see what we once were. Oh yes, we shall raise our ancient hosts to assist you. . . .

TWENTY-SEVEN

DUKE MODESET stood atop the tallest tower
of his palace, surveying the rebellion below through an
elegant telescopic device he'd found in the war room.

His manservant stood a little way behind him,
looking uncomfortable. "Sorry to keep on, milord,
but why am I standing on this trapdoor, again?"

The duke sighed.

"I've told you, Pegrand, in order to keep our most
energetic citizens from running me through with a
blade."

"But, I've locked it, milord, and I've jammed a crowbar through the handle."

"Yes, well, I'm not taking any chances. Now just stand still, will you?"

"Er . . . right, milord. Whatever you say."

Modeset returned his attention to the telescope, then collapsed it and put it away.

"We're in big trouble this time, old friend. You do realize that, even if the children miraculously come hurtling through the gates in the next five minutes, my days in this city are numbered."

"Oh, no, milord. Surely if—"

Modeset waved his manservant's protestations away.

"We have to face facts, Pegrand. Even if the parents forgive me, the Yowlers won't give up an opportunity to step in. They've wanted my blasted cousin for the throne ever since he was born. If I don't get murdered, at the very least I'll be sent into exile. Perhaps it might be best for all concerned if I just jump."

Modeset climbed up onto the nearest buttress and stretched out his arms like a man imitating a bird.

"B-b-but you can't—"

A sword blade suddenly shot up through the trapdoor, narrowly missing the manservant's privates.

"Um, right you are, milord," he gasped. "Don't hang about, now."

TWENTY-EIGHT

THE CAVERN was a hive of frantic activity. Children scrambled left and right, dodging and swerving to avoid the walking cadavers Diek had enticed from the cracked earth in an attempt to stop them leaving.

"Down! Down! Do-o-own!"

Gordo flew over the heads of the nearest children as if he'd been fired from a cannon, barreling into the undead mass with his battle-axe a blur. Skulls shattered and half-rotted limbs flew left and right, but the dwarf wasn't having things all his own way. An evil-looking gash had been opened on his forehead and several of the staggering grave walkers were clawing mindlessly at his back. With every triumphant blow, he darted frantic glances left and right, but Groan was nowhere to be seen.

Kill the sorcerer, boy. Destroy him.

Diek—his own mind long gone—made to focus his gaze on Tambor. This time, a plume of yellow fire flew from his hands and surged toward the sorcerer. It hit the rocky ledge beneath him, which in turn came away from the wall and crashed to the ground.

Diek smiled with satisfaction, and tried again. He sent a furious bolt of energy flying across the cavern, encased the old man and spun him around in midair, increasing in velocity until Tambor was nothing more than a blur. The spell intensified and the air began to hum. One more effort and. . . . Diek toppled backward, his concentration broken. The spell weakened as the sorcerer's attention was diverted to his own safety.

The boulder had moved. Diek peered over his shoulder, and saw the barbarian grinning up at him.

Groan was underneath the boy's temporary stage, employing his considerable strength to tip it over. He gave one final grunt of effort, and Diek fell. The spell withered and died.

Tambor plummeted downward. He still had enough awareness to roll as he hit the ground, but his own momentum took him over the edge of the promontory. His legs scrabbled for purchase on the rock face and he hung there, dangling precariously in midair.

Thanks to some lucky hacks and a small group of enthusiastic, rock-pelting teenagers, Gordo was winning his battle with the undead. Cutting down the last hideous corpse in his path, he paused to catch his breath before rounding up the remaining innocents. Not that there were many; the children had evidently decided pretty quickly that they didn't like the place they'd woken up in, and most of them had already begun to follow Jimmy toward the exit tunnel.

It was just as well; things were about to get a lot worse.

Tambor had managed to scrabble back onto his ledge. He got shakily to his feet and patted the dust from his robe. I'm too old for this, he thought, as he lowered himself down onto one creaky knee and began to recite another spell.

"Come on, you stragglers! Get through the tunnel!"

Gordo sighed; being three foot nothing didn't prepare you well for ordering children to follow you.

Farther along, Jimmy was having his own trouble maintaining order. He'd realized early on that the easiest way to control the situation would be to occasionally grab one kid, issue an instruction, and hope for the best. He reached out and grasped a jerkin.

"Hurry along," he snapped. "There's a terrible, er, five-headed troll coming!"

He looked down. A little girl with pigtails was trembling.

Calm down.

Diek was trying to dislodge The Voice from his skull. He clapped his hands over his ears and screamed.

Calm down!

He dropped to the ground, eyes suddenly devoid of soul.

Now, focus on the rock.

Groan wondered if the foreigner was lying behind the boulder, unconscious. He hoped he was. With an almighty effort, he put tremendous pressure on the rock and moved it forward a few feet. Then he let go, leaped back, and grimaced. The boulder was rolling toward him again, fast. He turned and ran.

Jimmy was having a hard time. He'd finally managed to assure the little girl with the pigtails that, no, there *wasn't* a terrible five-headed troll coming, but that they did still need to hurry. He'd carried her to the head of the line but had to put her down again because, surprisingly for a little thing with not an ounce of fat on her, she'd weighed a ton.

"Quiet down!" he boomed. A few sniggers broke out about twenty heads down the line.

"Mummy says you shouldn't shout at children," said the little girl.

Jimmy raised one eyebrow. "Mummy's not trapped inside a mountain," he said, then stopped abruptly. He'd expected a few surprises, coming out of a mountain with thousands of children. A portcullis hadn't been one of them.

It ran from wall to wall and blocked the path from floor to ceiling. He felt around for a lever but couldn't find one. He turned back to the girl.

"Does Mummy have anything to say on the subject of subterranean portcullises?" he asked.

"Dunno," said the girl. She sniffed. "Don't fink she's interested in that."

No, thought Jimmy, I bet she isn't. "Right," he said. "Stand back. I'm going to lift it."

He reached down and took hold of two squares in the iron lattice. Then he pulled with all his might. Nothing happened. A few small boys hurried up to help, but there was just no moving the thing.

Jimmy sighed. "Okay everyone," he started. "We'll have to go back. . . ."

"We will *not*."

Gordo appeared from behind the knees of a gangly teenager, and nudged his way up to the group at the portcullis. "Let's move this thing, shall we?" he said.

The dwarf clasped his gnarled hands around the squares of the grid, and began to haul with all his might. Again, a few eager teens lent some dubious assistance. At last, there was a slow and dreary creak. Then the portcullis began to grind upward. A small boy near the front cheered and clapped his hands. He was soon joined by others. Gordo didn't know why but, somehow, this made him feel about three inches taller.

"There's not much space," he breathed. "You, the girl with the pigtails, go through and see if there's a button you can push to lock this thing in place once we've raised it."

Despite Jimmy's protests, the little girl stepped forward. Then she hesitated.

"Mummy says—"

"I don't care. Just get through and do it!" Jimmy shouted.

The girl crouched down and crawled through the gap.

A few seconds later there followed a sharp click. It echoed off through the tunnel. Gordo breathed a sigh of relief and let go. The portcullis slid down again.

The rock had caught up with Groan Teethgrit and wedged the barbarian into a corner. He heaved his body at it, but the magical force driving it on was simply too powerful.

Tambor was halfway through his chant when he first consciously realized the power of the spell he was about to perform. This was no mere conjuration, this was the Doorway of Death. Once you'd cast it, there was definitely no going back. He didn't even know what was likely to happen, only that it might involve his . . . paying a price. Back in his days at the Elistalis, he'd heard plenty of the older pupils talking about it, and most of the fragmentary conversations he'd caught were worrying. Some said that a terrible creature arrived to claim the victim, while others warned that even the act of invoking the spell drained the life from the caster. Tambor gulped; that was a possibility he was just going to have to entertain. He began to invoke the last line of the chant.

On reflection, it hadn't been a bad old life really, full of exciting quests and astounding magical discoveries in the early days, full of . . . er . . . paperwork afterward. He came to the end of the spell, stopped, and felt the magic surge through him.

He pointed a finger at Diek Wustapha and prayed.

The spell took effect almost immediately.

There was a thunderclap, which resonated deep inside the base of the cavern, and a seam tore in the fabric of reality. Tambor gasped; he'd misjudged his positioning, and the portal hovered a short distance behind the foreigner, who was facing away from it, oblivious.

Maybe, thought Tambor, he'll just step back and stumble straight into it. He smiled wanly; it was wishful thinking, and he knew it.

Diek was raising the pressure on Groan, his face contorted with the gut-wrenching effort required to steer the magic in his mind.

Tambor took a deep breath, steeled himself, and began to climb down from his ledge to the cavern floor.

"What's the holdup?" shouted Jimmy, trying to peer past Gordo into the shadows beyond the portcullis. The dwarf had managed to lift the great gate once more, but he was groaning with the effort involved.

"Pigtails reckons she can't press the button properly," he called. "She's not tall enough. I know the feeling."

"I'll do it," said Jimmy, scrambling under the spikes that stabbed from the underside of the barrier. A click echoed through the tunnel, but this time Gordo waited a few seconds. Then he released his grip on the iron and stepped away. Mercifully, the portcullis stayed where it was.

Jimmy scrambled back through the gap. "See?" he said. "No problem. There might be a way out, too. She can see a light."

"Good."

Gordo turned back toward the congregation of faces. "Everyone follow me!" he shouted, and ducked under the portcullis.

"Right," said Jimmy. "I'm going back a bit to make sure we've got them all. Hopefully, we'll meet up again out in the open."

Groan Teethgrit pushed hard against the boulder, but Diek's unshakable concentration was closing the gap, fast. He felt as if he were trapped in a vise powered by the gods. The harder he fought, the more the pressure built, squashing, squeezing, crushing, until—

It stopped, suddenly and without any apparent victory on Groan's part. The barbarian eased himself from his crevice and lurched forward to see what had happened.

There was a fight going on.

From what little Groan could make out through the swirls of magic still crackling through the air, Tambor had barreled into the foreigner and was currently belting him with a bruised (but nevertheless effective) closed fist. The boy's face was progressing through a series of strange attitudes; he looked both demonic and furious. As Groan headed toward the scuffle, Diek shot up an arm which coursed with energy and sent the old man careering back across the cavern. He gazed admiringly at his own hands and flashed the approaching barbarian an otherworldly smile.

Good. Very good. You see? These people are no match for us.

Groan drew his sword, swung it back in a wild arc, and let go.

Diek caught the blade in midair, and tossed it aside. "Is that the best you can do?" he asked, his voice now exuding darkness.

Tambor struggled to his feet, screamed in frustration, and charged.

Diek gave an evil cackle and stepped aside, but he was a fraction too late to avoid contact completely. Tambor flew past, catching the boy with a heavy blow on the side of the head before he disappeared into the dark doorway amid a flurry of curses. There was a loud roar from beyond. The portal sizzled, as if in the process of digesting the old sorcerer. Then it began to close.

But Diek had lost his concentration. He staggered, reeling from the old man's blow, clutching his skull, and moaning.

He didn't see Groan.

The barbarian bolted across the cavern, his muscular legs pumping with furious energy. He reached the foreigner, snatched him up by the neck, and hurled him at the shrinking darkness.

Diek awoke from his reverie just in time to snake out a hand and grab the edge of the doorway, but it was too late.

The portal closed. The cavern fell silent.

The last wisp of stray magic faded away. Groan stood ready to fight, one eye on the space previously occupied by Tambor's doorway. I've gotta get myself a bigger sword, he thought.

TWENTY-NINE

"GOOD-BYE, DULLITCH! May all your future monarchs suffer the same hellish, vomitous luck that I've had to endure."

Modeset tilted forward on tiptoe, allowed himself one final glimpse of the city, and dropped, down . . . down . . . down. . . .

At this point, somewhere past the third floor, he landed on a flagpole, which propelled him back up at an alarming speed. He subsequently erupted through the wooden floor of a balcony on the fourth floor,

crashed the wrong way through its awning, clung frantically to the tattered remains of the same, swung into
the palace like a crazed monkey, and landed face first
on the floor of the throne room before Quaris Sands
and Burnie.

"Nice of you to drop by, milord," said the
troglodyte, ducking a brick that had followed the duke
in. "At least you're doing your bit to keep the crowd
entertained."

There followed an inevitable outburst of derisive
laughter, punctuated by some serious blasphemy from
the bruised duke. This petered out when the throne-
room door came crashing down, and a sea of enraged
parents poured in through the gap.

THIRTY

Somehow, because of a strange conjunction
of circumstances, Gordo found himself playing catch-
up. Since leaving the mountain, he appeared to have
lost the initiative. Children milled around him, push-
ing and shoving (in some cases without so much as an
apology). It seemed as though, via some basic instinct,
they knew the way home. Perhaps, Gordo thought, you
log stuff on some higher level when you're in a trance.
Remarkable.

Jimmy caught up with him. "Bit of luck, that
portcullis coming up easy," he said.

The dwarf scowled. "It wasn't luck and it wasn't easy! It was strength, boy. Never judge a man by his size."

"Strength? You think?"

"Yes. Do you want to make something of it?"

"No, of course not." Jimmy held up his hands in surrender. "I just wouldn't of thought it, that's all. You must be very, er, able."

Gordo nodded. "You ever hear of the time when Groan defeated the seven-headed dragon of Anzell Bay?"

"Hmm . . . I think so," Jimmy lied.

"I ripped the claws off it when he'd finished."

"Amazing," the thief muttered. "I bet that took some doing."

"Ha! It's no fun, I can tell you, manicuring a dragon. Grime gets right under your fingernails."

"No, I'm sure. Have you seen Stump, by any chance?"

"Your mate with all the hair? I thought he was with you."

Jimmy shook his head. "He fell down a chute or something."

"Ha! Silly sod. He'll be in that mountain for weeks!"

"Oi," shouted a voice.

Gordo and Jimmy tuned to see Groan emerging from the tunnel. The barbarian looked battered, bruised, and miserable. At least *he's* unaffected, thought Gordo. As the barbarian approached, Jimmy looked around him. "Where's Granddad?" he called.

There was a dreadful, dreadful silence. "'E's gone," Groan managed, at last. "Sorry."

Jimmy shook his head. "What do you mean 'gone'?" he asked, fighting back the first hint of a tear. "Where? How?"

Groan took a while to answer. "He went fru the doorway, took the foreigner wiv him."

"He was a brave man," said Gordo, patting the thief affectionately on the leg. "Those children may very well owe their lives to him."

"And us," added Groan, who was prepared to go so far with sympathy, but didn't want any sentimental issues interfering with his share of the reward.

A wind whistled on the mountainside.

"Looks like the children can't wait to get back," said Jimmy, trying not to show his sorrow. He was gesturing toward a group of thirty or forty youths who had wandered off the path to start a rock fight between the trees. "Bless them, eh?"

"Little demons," Gordo snapped.

"City owes us money," said Groan, with rancor.

Jimmy smiled at the thought of Modeset parting with gold; perhaps Dullitch's purse-string vigilante wasn't going to get away without a scratch after all.

"I wish I hadn't lost that horse," he said.

"So do we," Gordo muttered.

The thief shook his head. "No, I meant for the ride home."

"I like walkin'," said Groan. "More chance of a fight."

"Me too," added Gordo. "Nice fresh air in your lungs." He licked his lips. "I expect you'll be in for your granddad's fortune," he said, grinning. "The spell book, that is."

Jimmy sniffed, nodded. "Not my thing," he said. "There isn't a magical bone in my body, thank the gods."

They walked in silence for a while.

"Of course," Jimmy added, thoughtfully, "there was always his gold vortiga bracelet. That must be worth thousands."

There was another prolonged suppression of breath.

"You'll be after that, then?" said Gordo, slyly. "You being a thief and all."

Jimmy shook his head. "Not likely." He passed a grubby hand over his forehead. "He never wore it, but he always had it on him somewhere. In a pocket, under his hat, in a shoe; anywhere you'd care to mention. Personally, I reckon he used to hide it inside that magic carpet of his."

Groan looked up toward the summit of the Twelve, and wondered if it was worth going back.

THIRTY-ONE

THE PARENTS had sticks, cudgels, knuckle-dusters and, in one extreme case, a knife. And yet they didn't move an inch toward the duke. They didn't dare.

Vicious had emerged from beneath the royal throne and proceeded, very quickly, to go off his rocker. Unbeknownst to the duke, who thought the little mutt might be displaying some deep sense of loyalty, he was actually protecting his bone. The hideous, half-rotted thing was hidden underneath a collapsed tapestry just behind the door, and one of the parents had taken a step

261

in the wrong direction. It wasn't the growl that frightened them, because Vicious didn't growl. Instead, he made a noise like a yodeler gargling with acid, his eyeballs rolling right back into his head, spit flying from his maw in every direction.

Every weapon clattered to the floor.

The duke, who had finally mustered enough dignity to scramble to his feet, raised a shaking hand.

"I understand you people want some answers," he began. "But the fact is, I have none to give you. Myself and my officials"—he indicated Quaris and Burnie, who both gave very weak waves—"have done the best we can in the circumstances. Now, will you please go to your homes and await the return of your children. Or else, I will . . . give the command."

Hesitation. Doubt. Defiance.

Then was a series of mumbled discussions and, one by one, the parents began to shuffle from the room.

When the last of them had departed, Modeset breathed a sigh of relief and, stepping forward, carefully patted his little dog.

"Thank you for that, my friend," he said, turning back to the others. "You know, I think he understands—"

What happened next was a blur. One moment the dog was sitting beside Modeset, wagging its tail excitedly, and the next it was hanging off his throat.

THIRTY-TWO

S O THE CHILDREN of Dullitch returned, just in time for the duke—and there was much rejoicing. The streets were filled with thankful parents, happy sons, and joyful daughters. Quaris Sands threaded his way through the crowds, shaking hands with some of the fathers and winking at their excitable offspring in that patronizing way that only adults with no children seem to employ.

In the palace, Groan and Gordo were also getting

the red-carpet treatment. Strangely, they'd been prevented from entering the city through the main gate with the children. Instead, a group of guards had taken them, via a very tangled route, to the palace.

Now, they stood before the duke who, it seemed, was wearing some sort of padded collar support.

"The city of Dullitch is in your debt," Modeset announced, pouring two measures from an expensive-looking bottle and passing the flagons to Pegrand to distribute. "You shall receive a full pardon, and the freedom of Dullitch."

"We'd bedda," Groan muttered, snatching his drink and scowling at the duke's manservant. "I've 'ad a gutful o' this stinkin' city. Where's our money?"

Modeset edged his way around the desk. "What are you talking about? I gave Quickstint two hundred crowns!"

"Hah!" Gordo was first off the mark. "We never got that—the thief lost the horse before he found us. We haven't seen a single crown of your damn money!"

Modeset gave an impassive shrug. "I don't see how that's my problem."

"Oh, you don't? Maybe Groan and I should show you."

The duke began to twitch. "Where is the horse now?" he asked.

"That's it! I've had enough." Gordo took one last swig from his flagon and tossed it aside.

"Come, come," Modeset soothed. "There's no need to get excited, little fellow. It was merely a question."

"Yeah," Groan boomed, "and *this is merely a sword,* but it's *nearly* stickin' out the back of your bleedin' 'ead."

The duke flinched, but suddenly his confidence seemed to strengthen.

"Oh really?" he snapped. "Then step up, great warrior, for it seems we have little to talk about."

The hulking barbarian drew his blade, took a stride forward, staggered, and collapsed. His flagon clanked across the marble floor, spilling its contents.

Gordo watched his friend in amazement, but found himself too weary to help. His limbs felt like lead weights.

"Now!" Modeset cried.

Pegrand hurried over to the door, where a rope snaked through a heavy torch bracket. He yanked the knot free and a great iron cage clanked down over the two mercenaries.

Burnie the troglodyte struggled out from the tattered remains of the great palace curtains. He was holding a small glass vial.

"We can't hang around," he said. "The alchemists reckon these sleeping draughts never last more than a couple of hours."

"Very good. Pegrand, Quaris, and I will take the barbarian. Burnie, do you think you can manage the dwarf?"

"Just about."

"Right, then. To the dungeons!"

THIRTY-THREE

G ORDO GOLDAXE was drowning his sorrows with some ale he'd found in a dank corner of his cell. At least, it tasted like ale. He held the bottle up and regarded it critically. It certainly *was* a strange color. He had a feeling it was watered down or low on liquor content. Either way, it was totally failing to get him drunk.

A few seconds passed in silence. Outside, a half-moon glowed in the sky. Gordo put his feet up on the bench beside him. He was about to nod off when a tune rang out from the next cell.

"Is that you, Groan Teethgrit?"

"Yeah."

"What is it?"

"'S a flute."

"Where did you get that?"

"Fell outta the foreigner's robe when I 'ad 'im off the rock."

Gordo leaped off his bunk. "Throw it away," he shouted. "It's probably cursed."

"Wants to be," said Groan, continuing to produce a strangled tune from it. "I've a good mind to try an' get them rats back."

"If he didn't kill them," said Gordo, unhelpfully. "I hate this city. It's a flaming cesspit. These cells are like sewers."

"Fick walls, 'n' all," said Groan. "I spent a year tryin' 'o get out of 'ere once; no good, hard as iron. These dungeons run right under the road."

Clip clop. Clip clop.

Clip clop, clip clop.

It was coming from above. Gordo looked up to the roof grate, but he couldn't see anything but moonlight and shadows.

Clip clop.

Clop.

Clop.

Gordo jumped up and down, stretched left and right, but he still couldn't make anything out. In the next cell, Groan was up and padding across the stones.

"'Ere," said the low booming voice, after a time.

Gordo sighed. "What? What is it?"

"You 'member the 'orse that thief lost?"

"Of course! I'm hardly likely to forget it, am I?"

"It's standing in the street over my cell!"

"Don't be ridiculous."

"Well it *looks* like an 'eraldic horse to me. 'S got a fat saddlebag 'n' all."

"You don't seriously think it's the same animal!"

"Dunno. I reckon it might be a homin' horse. You know what I mean, one that comes back on its own accordion."

"Well, there's nothing we can do about it now," said Gordo doubtfully, and settled down to sleep.

Eventually, around midnight, Groan stopped trying to coax the horse within reach and took a nap himself. He dreamed of beautiful maidens, a bath full of soya milk, and a scrubbing brush. Like his partner, he slept peacefully. In a week or two, Gordo would come up with a daring plan and they'd make their escape. They always did. . . .

THIRTY-FOUR

T HE FOLLOWING morning, as Jimmy Quickstint entered the draughty chambers beneath Yowler House, several high-ranking dignitaries stared out at him from the depths of their swarthy hoods. The halls here were lined with fanciful tapestries, all hand-stolen from many of the wealthiest lords in Dullitch.

In the center of the room sat Riggor DeWatt, master of the Rooftop Runners for more than forty years. His face, like those of his colleagues, was concealed, but he wore a ring of such magnificence that his identity was obvious. It actually required two fingers to support it.

Jimmy reached the center of the chamber, and bowed low. "You asked to see me, sir?"

The hood looked up. Jimmy could just make out the shadowy form of a chin. "I did," came a booming, resonant voice. "Jimmy Quickstint—"

"Yes, sir?"

"Quiet! Jimmy Quickstint—"

"Sir?"

"Silence! I'm trying to pronounce you. *Jimmy Quickstint—*"

The thief tried to avert his eyes, while at the same time looking hopeful.

"Because of your bravery—"

"My bravery?"

"Your bravery," echoed the congregation of cowls.

"Your honor—"

"Honor? Really?"

"Your honor."

"And your loyalty to the crown—"

"To the crown."

There was a pause.

"We have decided against admitting you to our organization. Sadly, we do not think that honor, bravery, or loyalty in this arena are directions in which we feel bound to move. Please leave via the west door, depositing your yearbook and complimentary swag bag in the alcove provided. If you don't have these items about your person, you are advised that you are permitted five days to return them. You also, it seems, owe the city two hundred crowns, so we strongly suggest you begin your search for the royal steed immediately. Good day."

Jimmy raised a hand to protest, but he was suddenly snatched and frog-marched out through a nearby door. Before he could so much as kick out a leg, he was dragged along a draughty passageway, hauled up several flights of stairs, and deposited, face first, on the cold cobbles of Palace Street, where he lay in a crumpled heap, too tired to move and too depressed to think. After a couple of seconds an alley cat padded up to him and widdled in his ear.

EPILOGUE

DUKE MODESET stood trial for his "incompetent handling" of the series of events which subsequently came to be known as the "Ratastrophe Catastrophe." He was exiled, along with his trusted manservant, Pegrand, leaving the throne to one Viscount Curfew, a rather insipid young man whom the Yowlers were rumored to have firmly in their pocket. Under his reign, the city once again became a haven for thieves and assassins, but at least the children were safe (a silver statue of Diek Wustapaha was placed in the Market Square to ensure that they always behaved themselves).

Duke Modeset's expulsion did not mark the end of his relationship with Dullitch, for he would return, some seven years later, at a time when the city faced an even greater crisis. . . .

ABOUT THE AUTHOR

DAVID LEE STONE was born in Margate Hospital on January 25, 1978, son of Barbara Ann Stone and Henry "Harry" Cooke. He was educated badly and therefore cannot by law name any of the schools at which this occurred (though one of them actually burned down before being relocated somewhere else).

After leaving school, David worked as a customer service rep at a well-known retail outlet, and helped to bankrupt his mother's (then successful) real estate agency, before searching for employment elsewhere.

These days, David can usually be found hammering away at a keyboard somewhere along the swollen lip of Kent, England. Beyond this, very little is known of the author, though he does have a small wart on the end of his left index finger.

The Ratastrophe Catastrophe is the first novel of the Illmoor Chronicles. The next volume in the series is currently underway.

THANKS TO:

My mother: apart from giving me overwhelming support and encouragement since I began writing, she has patiently read and reread every chapter of this novel since it was started in 1996. She also found me the best agent in the business. *Sophie Hicks*, that very agent, for unswerving support and a faith that never faltered. Finally, I'd like to thank my British editors, *Venetia Gosling* and *Anne McNeil*, for buying Illmoor in the first instance; and my New York editor, *Liza Baker*, for her advice in editing the U.S. version of the book.

Look for the second installment of

THE ILLMOOR CHRONICLES

THE
YOWLER FOUL-UP

by DAVID LEE STONE

COMING SOON...

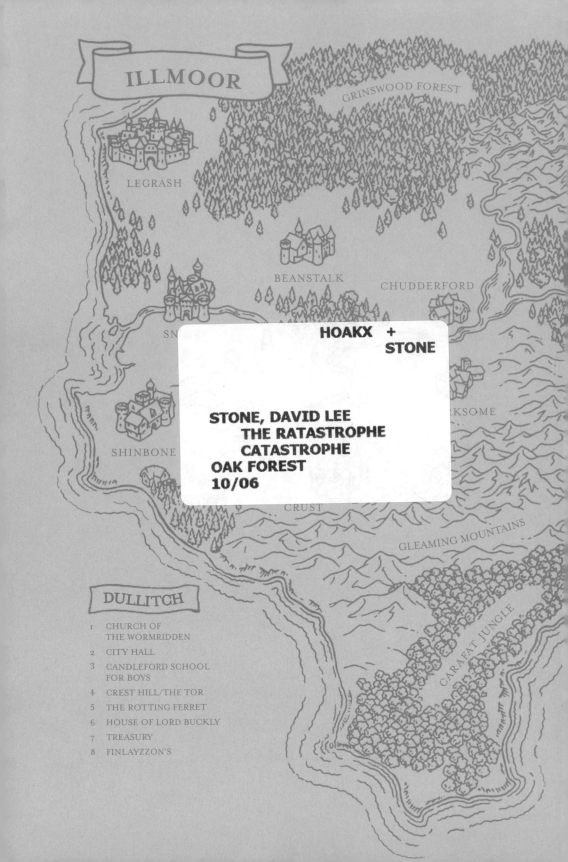